MACKENZY FOX

HUTCH

BARREN RIDGE REBELS MC
BOOK 11

DEDICATION

For those of you who were waiting patiently for this story.

You've been there since the beginning. Words can't express how grateful I am x

AUTHOR NOTE

CONTENT WARNING: Hutch is a steamy romance for readers 18+ it contains mature themes that may make some readers uncomfortable.

It includes violence, mentions of bullying, child abuse (not graphic, only mentioned) torture (don't worry, it's deserved) stalking, miscarriage (not detailed) coarse language…basically what the Bracken Ridge boys do best! And as always….LOTS of very spicy love scenes!

Things to note:

Hutch begins from when he and Kirsty first met (he's 22 and she's 18) the story begins in the past and slowly builds in order to show how Hutch worked his way through the ranks of the club, how they fell in love and so much more, until we're in the present day for the last chapters and the epilogue.

Bracken Ridge Demons was the original club name before Hutch was president and changed the name to Bracken Ridge Rebels

The siblings named Joshua and Amanda in the book are now known as Gunner and Summer

BLURB

HUTCH

I built this club from the ground up
Everything I've worked towards is here, I did this…
I made my club into something I can be proud of
The men, the women, the kids - they're all family
And family stick together
No matter what
Even when times get tough
Even when the good lord himself tests me
Even when he threatens to take things away
I won't relent. I won't ever give up on the ones I love
Especially her
My woman
My everything
Kirsty
I will fight to the bitter end, even if it may break me in the process

KIRSTY

There's never been a man like him
He's the one I dream of
Honest, brave, and good to the very core
He's the one I belong to
The only man that knows the heart of me…
But this is the one fight that he can't command
He can't twist and bend it his way
He can't predict the outcome
Some things are best left untouched
Some words are best left unspoken
Because if they are allowed to break free
I don't know if either of us will survive the fallout
Not this time

Bracken Ridge Rebels rule…enter at own risk!

BRACKEN RIDGE
REBELS
ARIZONA
M · C

CHAPTER 1

HUTCH

AGED 22

I thank the server as they hand me my daily fix of coffee, just the way I like it, then make my way out of the cafe and toward my sled, parked at the curb. Just as I'm leaving, I almost run into the young blonde woman coming through the door.

I jerk back. Holy shit.

I'm about to go off, having almost spilled my coffee all over myself, and her, but then our eyes meet.

Holy fucking shit. She's cute.

I close my mouth. I don't swear at or toward women at the best of times. The only time I do is if I'm going to pound town and she's into it, but most chicks around here aren't into foul mouths while fucking, unfortunately.

I raise my eyebrows. "Well, well, little lady, that'll teach me to watch where I'm going."

She's got the prettiest blue eyes I've ever seen. Fair

skin, no makeup, blonde curly hair that sits just below her chin. I can't say much for her body, as she's covering it up with a big, baggy sweatshirt and oversized jeans, but she's curvy as fuck…and I like it. I'm not into skinny women. A man needs something to hang on to while he's giving it his all.

And I'd certainly like to…

"It's fine…" she says, not meeting my eyes, then she immediately looks down at the ground.

Fuck. She's shy? Oh, this is gonna be good.

"Not really, I could've scalded you."

"I doubt it."

She still looks anywhere but at me.

"Haven't seen you around here before," I say, running a hand through my hair.

Nope. I'd remember her anywhere.

Like clockwork, her eyes slowly rise, and she watches the movement.

I keep myself in good shape. I lift weights and I've got tattoos. Her eyes flick to my bicep as I palm the back of my head, a small smirk playing on my lips.

Chicks dig the smirk.

They dig my cock too, but let's not get into that right now. I'm enjoying myself just looking at her.

I got my looks from my mama. My temper from my dad. Not that I wanted to inherit anything from that bastard, but at least I know when to use it.

Mama had it tough, but we all did in that household. I don't speak to my brother, or my sister. Some shit that happens during your childhood just stays there once you leave, never to be spoken of ever again. Mama had it the worst, though.

When my dad passed away suddenly from a heart attack, it was like a fucking miracle.

"I've lived here for about a month," she says quietly. "I mean, my parents bought a business, and we all moved."

How old is she? She's gotta be older than eighteen… Fuck. Please, be older than eighteen.

"No shit?"

She bites down on her bottom lip, and I feel my cock twitch.

Her lips are round and plump and, without a stitch of lipstick on, it makes me want to bite down on them.

She nods, but doesn't say anything else as we maneuver around one another, so she's now in the entry and I'm half outside, keeping the door wedged open with my boot.

Her eyes graze over my club patch at the front of my cut.

Bracken Ridge Demons. I'm part of a one percent club that is notorious in this town. I prospected young. I'm only twenty-two, but I've been around the block a time or two. I'm wiser than I probably look, not that it matters, pussy is pussy.

"Well," she stammers. "I'd better…uh…get going."

Again, she avoids looking at me.

I chuckle. "It was nice to meet you…" When she doesn't offer me her name, I prompt. "I'm Richie, by the way, but my friends call me Hutch."

She smiles, and holy shit if my cock doesn't jump in my jeans.

I hold my hand out, and her eyes go slightly wide as she glances at it. I have rings on every finger, including my thumbs, and bracelets stacked on my wrists, along with my grandpa's watch.

I want to touch her, but this will have to do for now.

"Are we friends?" She frowns, a small smile still playing on her lips.

I lean toward her, still holding my hand out as she takes it. "Honestly? I'd like to be a lot more." I give her a wink.

Her eyes go slightly wide as we shake. Her hand is small, soft and dainty in my large, warm one.

She opens her pretty mouth, then closes it again.

Her cheeks are flushed, and a red blush works its way up her neck.

Has this chick honestly never been complimented before? That's a damn shame.

I can even overlook the dowdy clothes she has on. I can see past that, and I'd bet that she has a smoking hot body under all those layers.

She lets go, brushing her hand up to her hair, tucking it behind her ear nervously.

I don't know why I like the fact I make her fucking nervous, but I do. Yet, I don't want her to be afraid of me. That's the last thing I want.

"Aren't you gonna tell me your name, darlin'?" I ask again as she starts to turn away.

My eyes bore into her as I give her my best shit-eating grin…and it works.

"Kirsty," she says in a small voice, the heat really rising to her cheeks now.

"I'll be seein' you around." I give her a chin lift, then close the door behind me.

Drinking my coffee, I head over to my sled. I mount it, but don't start it yet.

My motorcycle may be a vintage Harley, but I've put a lot of work into it and basically all of my money. I've always loved tinkering around with machinery and engine parts, so I fixed it up in my spare time.

I glance toward the coffee shop windows, the floor-to-ceiling glass, and I see Kirsty still staring at me.

I smile to myself.

Bingo.

Got her attention.

I finish my coffee, ditching it in the nearby trash can as I start the engine.

The straight pipes are loud. People stop and stare whenever any of the boys ride through town, but my bike is the loudest. I wear that shit like a badge of honor.

I'm proud of it, even if my club treats me and each other like shit. It's not how I would run things if I were Prez.

I rev the engine a few times, turning my head back to the window. When our eyes meet again, I give her another smirk, so fucking sure of myself and, without missing a beat, I take off from the curb like a bat out of hell, knowing she's still watching, and that excites me all the more.

I want her.

I know nothing about her, but I want her.

I like her shyness, her sweetness. She's nothing like the chicks I know at the club.

Nobody ever says no to me. Nobody.

It's the face.

But she's got my attention, loud and clear. As I ride down the street and out of eyeshot, I adjust my throbbing cock through my jeans. I gotta take care of that. I only hope to God she wants to get to know me like I do her.

When I get back to the clubhouse, just in time for the meeting, Spyder slaps me on the back as I enter through the door.

"Where you been at?"

I don't like him, but then again, I don't like a lot of the brothers and how they treat each other, not to mention women. But since I'm only recently patched in, I've gotta ride the wave until I gain some respect from them. Not that I want Spyder's respect in any way, shape, or form, but here we are.

"Balls deep in pussy," I say, because that's the only thing he'll buy without trying to poke his nose in where I don't want it.

The last thing I want is him knowing I've got a new conquest in my sights.

Kirsty is a no-go area for any of my brothers. I may have just met her, but that doesn't mean I don't want to know more. I also don't want her coming around the club.

Shit gets awful real around here and she's too young and innocent to deal with that.

It's a red flag that I should stay away from her, but I'm not used to women who don't jump my bones. It's a new experience for me.

He tugs me closer as we walk toward the meeting room. "Anyone we know?"

I shrug. "Some dumb bitch."

He grins. "Taught you fuckin' well, brother. Treat 'em mean, keep 'em keen, just like I told you."

Spyder's a fuckhead. He taught me nothing.

One day, I'll put my hands on him and put him in his place, but today isn't that day.

We all know what this meeting is about. More drugs. More guns. More fucked-up shit; that's what this club is all about. The club coffers aren't exactly flowing at the moment, but our club Prez, Scar, will do anything to make sure they are.

I might only be twenty-two, but the brothers don't push me too hard. I'm one of the tallest in the club, despite my age. And I fight dirty. I fight any which way I have to in order to win.

If shit goes down, I make sure I'm the last man standing. I guess if my dead-beat dad taught me anything, it was how to put up a good fight.

The rest of his bullshit was not worth wiping my ass on.

I glance around the table at some of my brothers.

Skull, the Vice President.

Freak, who is exactly how he sounds, the club's Sergeant at Arms.

Harlem, the club's Enforcer.

Rainman, the Treasurer.

Road King, the Road Captain.

I'm just a member; though, most of the guys in this club are about past their expiry date.

I hope to gain a position soon, even if some of the guys will probably never leave this club unless they're in a body bag.

I can't honestly say Scar does anything on the up and up. It's not how he operates, nor the club.

The club takes what it wants, when it wants. Fuck the residents or anyone who tries to get in our way.

The cops have been at the Demons for years, watching closely, trying to pin anything and everything on us. But so far, Scar and the majority have managed to stay on the other side of the law. Some of the cops in this town are in our pockets, but shit's changing all the time.

Times are getting tougher, though. And that means things are getting more desperate.

At church, the majority may vote one way, but Scar has that knack of being able to push the boys into doing exactly what he wants.

He knows psyche 101 to a tee, and most people are afraid of him.

He's intimidating, I'll agree on that. But most of all, he has that power of authority where people listen to him.

I should be all about my Prez, and I have his back in many ways, but seeing where this club is headed, it's weighed heavily on my mind for some time.

But time is all I have. And I have to hold out until I can rise from the ashes.

I'm not staying a member for much longer. I want to grow in the ranks, I want to be somebody. Kicking the dirt and bouncing on the bones of my ass ain't fun.

Shit costs money, and I'm not the only one getting restless.

One day, I'm gonna be Prez of this club. One day, it'll be me sitting at the helm, commanding everyone's attention. One day, I will have my own empire, and all of this will seem like a distant memory.

I just gotta bide my time.

And I can't wait for that day to come.

BRACKEN RIDGE
REBELS
ARIZONA
M·C

CHAPTER 2

HUTCH

We take a seat with the others as Scar sits at the helm, waiting for him to begin.

Scar has been Prez for years, long before I was a prospect.

He's old, sixty maybe, and set in his ways.

I'm cocky most of the time, I admit that, but the old ways of running a club don't seem to be working. Everyone is on tenterhooks, and rightly so. We all need to get paid.

None of us are in this for love. No, it's all about pay dirt and chicks. And club business always comes before pussy.

"First order of business," Scar begins. "Nail, where the fuck did you get that fuckin' haircut?"

We all turn to Nail, who's sitting in the back. Some dumb shit gave him a mo-hawk. Fuck's sake.

"Your mother," he yells back, amidst more chuckles.

Scar flips him the bird.

"We've got a new shipment comin' this week. As we all know, coffers have been fairly unimpressive for a while and this is our pay dirt, boys. Got some good clean shit we can cut. Was thinkin' we could take a ride out to Mesa and Phoenix. Once word gets out on the street this shit is gold, everyone's gonna want it."

We cut cocaine and make it into crack. Not exactly rocket science, but it's one way to make coin.

None of this happens at the clubhouse. The club has a number of houses around town, where some of the brothers, who are experienced in mixing and cutting agents, will dissect it and make different compounds, depending on how much they have to work with.

Judging by Scar's face, it's a substantial amount.

I never knew much about street drugs until I joined the club.

The goal as dealers is always to keep the customer hooked and buying, that's number one. There's three ways of doing this.

Intensifying the high and getting the customer hooked so they'll come back for more.

Followed by cutting the next stash, using a less potent cutting agent so they'll buy more to chase the same high as before, never fully reaching it. By this stage, they're addicted.

And then finally, mixing the coke with meth, making it even more potent and more addictive.

The latter depends on how much of a supply there is and

if there's more readily available. Usually, that's not the case, hence why we're living like fuckin' paupers.

I've never touched the hard stuff myself. That shit'll fuck you up. Maybe I've seen too much crazy shit in my short life, but dope, booze, and pussy are what do it for me.

Seen too many overdoses, and I don't wanna see another if I can help it.

Disturbing doesn't even describe it.

I'm just glad I'm not cutting the stuff. I wouldn't wanna be the guy who mixes a lethal cocktail and be responsible for the consequences.

As long as I get a slice of the pie, have pussy hanging off my arm, and cash in my pocket, I don't want for much else.

I don't believe in the institution of marriage, not after seeing what my own parents did with it and what my mom went through. Fuck that shit.

Life's too short. I'm here for a good time, not a long time.

I don't know why an image of Kirsty flashes through my mind at that thought.

She's a conquest, nothing more.

I like how she looked at me, slightly startled, like I was an anomaly.

I've never had a woman not try to throw themselves at me, and truth be told, it was kinda refreshing.

I'm used to women being very forward. Stripping in front of the other brothers, not giving a shit who sees them. Hell, most of the brothers fuck wherever they can, and they don't give a shit who's watching. Those are the kinds of women who hang around the clubhouse.

Easy women.

You don't have to do shit to get them in your bed.

But Kirsty…she was shy, also something else I'm not used to, and sweet.

She's far too innocent for me. Again, I start to hope she's over eighteen. I don't mess with that shit. Woman's gotta be legal.

She's also gotta be into me.

With Kirsty, I think she was more curious than anything.

There's no way a woman like her would go for a guy like me in the real world, and that poses a challenge in itself.

Aside from the fact she had zero confidence, and she couldn't look me in the eye for longer than a few seconds, I'm definitely interested.

Maybe it's the chase.

Maybe it's because of those eyes, so fuckin' beautiful, they blew me away.

Or perhaps it's those soft, delicious looking lips that would look fantastic wrapped around my cock.

I should leave her well enough alone. I don't need to

pursue her, but I know I'm going to.

Because of the way she acted, it's now a challenge.

I look up, realizing Skull is looking at me and he just asked a question.

Did he mention the van? And when it'll be back from the mechanics?

Yeah, I think so.

The van is at the body shop after one of the Prospects rammed it into a guardrail.

"Thursday, they're findin' it difficult gettin' the fender out of the carburetor," I say, hoping that was the question.

Chuckles sound throughout the room.

"Fuck's sake," Scar mutters as Skull gives me a chin lift.

"Money don't fuckin' grow on trees," Rainman agrees, always thinking about the bottom line. "If anyone's got any suggestions, other than using a cage, none of which are reliable enough to make a trip to Costco, let alone Phoenix, then let me know."

"Already on it," I go on, trying not to let my ego get the better of me. This played out exactly how I wanted it to; in my favor. "Secured a cheap van a friend lent me until we've got ours fixed. The thing's old, but runs fine, not so conspicuous either. Even has an old business logo on the side; Jim's Auto Dealers. It'll do the job."

When I said I'd do just about anything to get ahead, I

wasn't kidding.

I definitely don't wanna be cutting coke, though. And I also don't wanna be responsible for selling shit to some kid who'll get hooked and maybe even OD. That shit doesn't sit well with me, but I prefer not to think about it.

"Thank fuck someone came to work today," Scar says as I feel every set of eyes on me from around the room. "Nice work, Hutch."

I shrug like it's nothing.

I don't give a shit what they think or if it seems as if I'm blowing smoke up Prez's ass. We wanna get paid, and without a van, we can't move the shit. If we can't move the shit, we don't get paid. Pretty fuckin' simple.

I wish half the dipshits in this club would meet me halfway, but none of them seem to have any drive or ambition. The only one remotely on the same page, aside from Scar and Skull, is Harlem, the club's Enforcer, so that goes without saying.

He's gotta be a certain way in the club to keep order and earn respect. If only the rest of the men in this room could be so lucky.

"Whose dick did you have to suck to organize that?" Freak pipes up.

I don't even spare him a glance. "Your mother's."

More chuckles.

"Funny fucker," Freak mumbles.

"If anyone else has any better ideas?" Scar says, glancing around the room.

"I don't see you makin' plans to get this shit on the road, Spyder, nor you, Road King. This batch is fuckin' hot, and we're gonna need to offload it fast." He looks at me. "Consider yourself upgraded from shitkicker to van driver."

Not exactly the promotion I was hoping for, but I'll take it.

I give him a chin lift. "Appreciate it."

I'd rather drive the getaway van than have to take part in the exchange itself. So much shit can go wrong. I don't wanna be in a fuckin' body bag at twenty-two because some dumb fuck thought he could take me.

Best to stay out of the firing line and the van is the perfect decoy.

I can see scowls aimed at me from all angles and knives practically being thrown at my back.

Scar needs to cull the ranks soon enough and I'll be ready.

There's no way I'm gonna be a van driver for the rest of my life, but it's a step up from taking out the garbage. Things will look up soon.

Bide your time. That's all you gotta do.

I'm going places.

Sometimes that might also mean biting my tongue, and I admit it's something I'm not great at. It shouldn't be a problem, really, since growing up all I did was bite my goddamn tongue, because if I didn't, I would have ripped my father's throat out.

I know I get my temper from him, and I've had years and years of practice at that too.

Some things never change, but I'll be fucked if I'm gonna resemble anything like him.

No goddamn way.

"The rest of you dumb fucks, let's get this shit moving." He points at Freak. "You got an update yet on our first supplier?"

He nods. "Got it under control, meetin' with him later today."

Scar frowns, turning to Skull. "You knew about this?"

Here we go.

"Was about to bring it up," he says coolly.

There's no love lost between these two. I always thought Skull would've made a better Prez than Scar, but as long as Scar's breathing, it's not gonna happen.

The trouble with this club, amongst many other things, is that there's no communication.

I might still be young and 'wet behind the ears,' as the older members like to say about me, but I'm street smart. I know that without communication, none of this shit's gonna happen quickly.

"Why do I feel like I have to fuckin' organize everythin' myself around here. If you had pussy right in front of you,

you wouldn't know what to do fuckin' with it," Scar says, as Skull pretends to ignore him.

"Speakin' of which, the party for Dog's fiftieth is next weekend," Grim, one of the brothers, interjects. "Thought we could all put in and get him a coupla strippers, might make him feel better about not bein' able to get it up anymore."

I snort a laugh, as do most of the men around the room. Dog has been complaining lately about how he never gets laid, so this could be good for him.

I can't even imagine getting that old and not being able to work my dick anymore. The thought makes me shudder.

"Not a bad idea. Could probably use a little entertainment around here," Scar agrees. "Set it up. I'm sure we can scrounge to get him some cheap pussy, nastier the better. But keep the pretty ones for me."

That's the only way a man like Scar can get any pussy. He lives up to his name, having a huge scar across his face from a bar room brawl some years back.

He's skinny, with a decent build, and has these weird gray, glassy eyes that make him look like he's a ghost. Let's just say, he's lived a full life.

"Speakin' of Dog, haven't seen you gettin' much snatch lately, either," Road King pipes up. "Maybe you need to start a charity for the Bracken Ridge geriatrics club. They're lookin' for new members."

Grim torpedo's the paper plane he's been making at Road King's head with force.

"Gettin' more pussy than you, brother, just ask your little sister."

Road King goes to stand, but Harlem pushes him back down.

"Don't be stupid," Harlem says, shaking his head. "He's bigger than you."

Road King mutters something about keeping Grim in line, but shrugs Harlem off.

Grim isn't the smallest of men. But even if his name suggests he's mean, he's actually one of the better brothers with a sense of humor, and only goes for the jugular when it's completely necessary. When he does, that shit's scary.

Scar also allows not just committee members of the club, but patched members into church, something I don't necessarily agree with. Meeting room tables are supposed to be about making decisions with those most trusted, before it goes through to the patched members. I wouldn't trust Spyder here, for example, as far as I could throw him. He'd sell his own grandmother to get ahead of you in the line.

But as I say, this is all experience for when I move up the ranks. I'm taking it all in, like a sponge.

"If you're finished bickering, we got work to do. Hutch, bring the van to the workshop. Scrooge will give it a once over to make sure it's roadworthy."

"On it."

"The rest of you know what needs to be done. We'll reconvene tomorrow. I need that list of suppliers, Freak, and I wanna be sure no fuckin' pigs are hangin' around. They get wind of any new shit comin' through town, they'll be all over us like a rash."

"I'll send them some donuts," Freak replies. "Keep 'em occupied the old-fashioned way."

Scar shakes his head in exasperation as I try not to laugh.

And that's exactly why I know I'm gonna be someone someday, because this is my competition.

Fuckin' donuts.

I run a hand through my hair. I've got work to do.

And one thing I know how to do other than play hard, is work hard.

I'm good at that.

I'm one up on everyone else because of the van, so now I just need to sit tight and stay outta trouble…if I can help it.

BRACKEN RIDGE
REBELS
ARIZONA
M · C

CHAPTER 3

HIRSTY

He's not at the cafe the next day, much to my disappointment.

I don't know why that thought even enters my head.

Richie Hutchison is not a good man.

Of course, I know who he is. Everyone in this town knows who he is.

He might be a sexy man, with very pretty eyes, and an amazing body…and that hair…but he's bad news. Everyone knows it, and as if that wasn't bad enough, he runs with the local biker club.

The Demons are not people you want to mess with or have a problem with. Rumor has it that the businesses around here pay them a fee to keep things in order

Protection money. It kinda sounds like the mafia, if you ask me.

The way Richie Hutchison looked at me the other day, though… I can't stop thinking about it.

He's something else, and he knows it.

That smug little smirk probably gets him anything he wants in the world. He probably doesn't even have to snap his fingers and the girls come running. He's very sure of himself, which is nothing like the boys I'm used to. Not that I would know because I've never even spoken to a boy, other than in class, and even then, it's out of obligation on their part. I've never been kissed or done anything remotely close to making out.

My parents are religious and very strict. We just got to town, after moving twice in one year.

My father wants to settle and they chose Bracken Ridge, being it's small, cozy and has that old-world charm that's missing these days.

But, I can't think of anything else, only that Richie "Hutch" should not be looking at me like that and, for some unfathomable reason, I liked it.

I liked how his eyes skimmed down my body, as if he enjoyed what he saw, which is ridiculous. He couldn't possibly. I'm not a small girl. I have a small waist, but that's the only thing little about me. My hips and ass are round and plentiful, my breasts too, from when I hit puberty. Being the butt of all the boys' jokes, I've always been self conscious of them.

I've always dressed in oversized clothes because I know I'm bigger than most girls, and I don't like to stand out.

Blending in is kind of my thing.

I'm not body confident like some of my friends. I don't like to show my body off because I'm embarrassed.

Maybe I was just imagining it, or maybe Richie was just playing with me because that's how he gets his kicks. My face starts to heat just thinking about it.

That's what it is. A joke. I'm a joke to him, just like I am with all the other boys I've ever known. They never looked at me twice, only to laugh or make fun of my outfit, or remind me how big my breasts are.

We don't have a lot of money, so my mom makes a lot of mine and my sisters' clothes.

Darlene is the pretty one, the girl who has it all. She's a year older than me, so she asserts that authority any chance she gets.

We've never been close, and now that she's off to college, doing her own thing, I've got a slight reprieve from her comments and ridicule.

I've decided to go to school to get my real estate license, rather than college, much to my parents' dismay. They had high hopes I'd get a scholarship, like my perfect sister, and become something like a doctor or a lawyer. They know I have the smarts for it, but that has never interested me. I hated school at the best of times, but I've always loved figures and learning how to make money. I also love real estate, I always have, so I've applied to intern at Bracken Ridge Real Estate while I complete my course. I want to learn the ropes from the bottom up, prove my parents wrong. Hopefully in time, I'll at least have some knowledge under my belt.

I tie my hair up. It's the one asset, aside from my eyes, that I actually like.

Naturally light blonde with a slight wave, it's wash and wear. I've always been pale, but I'm a little more tan since moving to the desert.

By Friday, I've forgotten all about Hutch and his wayward eyes. It's my second day on the job at the real estate office and the first task they give me is picking up morning tea from the cafe, along with eight cups of coffee that I'm somehow supposed to balance on my head.

It's a nice day outside. Springtime is lovely here, not too hot and the sun doesn't burn you to a cinder.

I'm dressed in my usual attire; pants, loafers, a baggy blouse, and a cardigan in case it gets cold. I make sure everything that sits on my body is loose and not too tight.

I love my sweats, but I can't exactly wear those to the office.

The cafe is all but deserted and I take a seat at one of the booths near the counter after placing the order.

Mindlessly perusing the menu, I think about my day ahead, wondering if my boss will show me anything that doesn't involve me running around doing errands.

I think about the fight I had with my mom this morning because she doesn't like Callie and Helen, the girls I'm hanging with from school. I don't know what she has against them. Okay, Callie may be a little on the wild side, but she's one of the few who have been nice to me since we moved here. Helen is studying to be a nurse, and Callie, being a year older, flunked out of school and is waitressing at the Heebie Jeebie.

I think at this point, my parents hate my life choices so much that anything I do won't have the desired effect they want for my life. Even if I was about to become the First Lady, I'm sure they'd find fault with it.

I don't look up when the seat next to me moves. I should have known better, because the second that musky, spicy smell invades my nostrils, I know it's not the server cleaning up.

My eyes raise from the menu as Hutch leans against the back of the stool next to me, that boyish grin on his face as he runs a hand through his tousled strands, a cigarette sitting behind one ear as I stare at him in shock.

Holy heck, he's attractive.

I feel a pulse in my lower abdomen, and my throat starts to thicken.

"Kirsty," he drawls, like it's a surprise to see me. "How nice to see you again."

I swallow hard, finding my mouth is stuck, and no

words are forming.

He looks down at my hands fiddling with the menu. I drop it quickly, shoving my hair behind my ears nervously.

"Hello, Richie."

This makes him grin even more. "You remembered my name?"

He leans over on the chair. Today he has a leather motorcycle vest on…and nothing underneath it. My eyes almost bulge out of their sockets when I see his muscled chest, tattoos peeking out in various colors…in fact…is that an eagle?

His body is absolutely insane, and I know I'm eyeballing him and probably have drool coming out of my mouth.

"I…uh…" I stammer, my eyes finding his again. I feel the heat rise in my cheeks once more. For heaven's sake, Kirsty, pull yourself together! "Um, yeah, I guess."

It's not like I could forget him. He's a force of nature.

"Is it because I'm so charming?" His eyes dance with mischief.

Oh, he knows he's all that.

No, it's the ass, the body, the eyes…the way he hangs on every word…the way he's looking at me now.

I try to clear this fog in my brain. I'm not like this. I'm smart. I've had to be the smartest person in the room because I didn't get looks and a body like my sister.

Everyone loves the smart, fat girl; she's the one who you can rely on, especially when there's an essay due and you want people to like you.

Why was I such a loser in high school? I feel like since graduation, I've grown up so fast and actually acquired a backbone.

"No, it's because you're part of the Bracken Ridge Demons, and you're barely wearing any clothes," I blurt out. Instantly, I slap my hand over my mouth.

What the hell?

He strokes his chin, like he has all the time in the world to stand here and interrogate me.

I glance over his shoulder to see how my order's doing, and I catch the server eyeing Hutch's ass. She hasn't even started boxing the pie up yet…I guess I wasn't far off about women fawning all over him.

"Nice of you to notice."

I look down at my hands.

"So, how are you?" he presses when I don't answer. "Since you almost spilled my coffee on me."

My eyes dart to his again, and I can't help but smile as I shake my head. "You ran into me, remember?"

He shakes his head slowly. "I don't think so, sweetheart."

Sweetheart? Oh, dear God.

"You don't seem like the coffee drinking kinda guy,"

I find myself saying, even though I should never open my mouth ever again.

"I think you'd find out a lot of things that would surprise you if you really knew me. For example, I wrestle mountain lions just for fun."

"You do not."

"Do too. I also got speared by a bow and arrow one time."

I shake my head, trying not to laugh. "I find that hard to believe."

"It's true, just ask my brother. The little jerk would do anything to try to knock me off just so he could steal my bedroom."

I laugh, tucking my hair again, avoiding his gaze.

"You've got pretty eyes, baby girl, but I gotta ask somethin'?"

Baby girl? I press my thighs together.

Uh oh.

I look up at him again, his eyebrows knitted together. "Yes?" Do I really want to know?

"Why do you wear these big, baggy sweaters? It's almost eighty degrees outside."

I blink once. Twice. Looking away quickly, I realize this is it. The joke.

He's here to taunt me, nothing more. Just like everybody else.

He's an asshole.

I mumble something incoherent as I start to stand. I need to get out of here. I need to get out of here now.

"Kirsty?" he says, when I don't answer. He cages me in, pressing his hand against the end of my chair so I can't escape. "What did I say?"

"I just…I just need to go."

"Why?"

"I…" I look anywhere but at him.

Then, my chin burns as he touches me there with one finger, tilting my chin up to face him.

In a softer tone, he asks, "What did I do?"

I shake my head.

"Kirsty?" His tone is more demanding now, and I feel my legs turn to jelly, and for some unfathomable reason, I'm wet between the legs. I can feel my arousal and I don't know what to do with that or why this man unnerves me so much.

"Is that what this is?" I stammer, my eyes having nowhere to go except to meet his.

"Is that what what is?" he counters, his eyes soft. Gosh, they're so blue…so sparkling…so pretty. He's too pretty to be a biker. His face has a small amount of facial hair, like he's trying to grow it out. That does things to me too.

"Did you just come here to make fun of me?" It takes me a few moments to get all the words out, and I feel my face burning.

He frowns, looking genuinely concerned. "Because I asked you about why you wear big sweaters?"

"Precisely."

His eyes are intense, but he doesn't let me look away, holding his finger in place. I wet my lips, and his eyes dart down to my mouth.

Holy shit balls…stop this!

My nipples peak, my core starts to throb, and I know I'm going to combust if I stand here any longer under his scrutiny.

"First, Kirsty, the reason I asked is because I think you're the most beautiful woman I've ever seen, with the prettiest eyes and mouth." My eyes go wide. "Second, I like your attitude. It's turnin' a little on the snarky side right now, but I can overlook that. Third…" His eyes skate down my body once more. "I bet you have a sexy body under all those layers, you just don't know how to show it off properly."

I press my thighs together as I try not to pant.

I don't even pretend anymore, closing my eyes as he moves his mouth to my ear, where he whispers, "I dream about what you'd taste like."

I bite down on my bottom lip, my hands starting to shake.

"Stop," I whisper.

His mouth still close to my ear, his scent invades me, taking over all rational in my brain. He grunts a laugh. "Do you really want me to?"

No! I want to feel your mouth on me…

I don't answer. I can't. I'm in too much of a state.

I put my hands on his chest, in an attempt to shove him off, but instead, it sends a fire to my core like nothing I've ever experienced. Desire, in its purest form.

But I don't want this.

I can't.

He looks down at my hands on his chest and makes a guttural grunt in the back of his throat. "I'm here, baby girl, and I see you," he says. "I see you."

I can't hear any more. I push past him and scurry out of the cafe, not even stopping to see where my order is, then I high-tail it up the street back to the safety of the office.

Once inside, I lean against the door and sigh out loud.

This isn't fair.

I won't let Richie Hutchison do this to me.

Dashing to the bathroom, I dab water on my face and sort out the mess I've made in my panties. I'm thoroughly disgusted with myself…I've never had a reaction to a boy like that before…except Hutch is no boy. He's a man, a man with a very dirty mouth.

I dream about what you'd taste like.

I close my eyes and count to ten, praying that the good Lord will save me and forgive me for my sins. All I'm doing right now is picturing him naked, with his head between my legs…I don't think I can Hail Mary my way out of that.

I stare in the mirror and shake my head.

He had to have been kidding.

I'm not beautiful.

I'm not sexy.

I'm not any of those things.

I'm stupid to think he meant them or that I'm anything special.

I shake it off, patting my face dry with a paper towel, hoping the redness will subside soon.

After about ten minutes, I leave the bathroom and walk toward my boss's office, about to explain why we don't have any coffee or morning tea…then I see one of the office girls, Cindy, biting into a muffin.

My eyes go wide. "Where did you get that?" I stammer, seeing the tray of coffees on the side, too.

"Oh, some biker dude dropped them off. Hey, weren't you supposed to collect them?"

I don't answer. I excuse myself back to the safety of my desk, where I can hide. Hopefully not just for the rest of the day, but for the rest of time.

BRACKEN RIDGE
REBELS
ARIZONA
M · C

CHAPTER 4

HUTCH

With my hand wrapped around my cock, I jerk it like a man possessed.

I don't know what the hell is wrong with me. I actually think I like this chick.

Well, that's obvious, since I'm jerking myself off instead of having one of the sweet butts take care of me.

I don't know what possessed me to tell her what I did, but I felt it was only right I let her know. It was like she has absolutely no clue how cute she is.

Something about her screams at me that there's a woman under those clothes, begging to be let out.

I mean, I wasn't lying.

She's beautiful. Her face…it's like an angel's. Her eyes kill me, and those lips…I squeeze harder, imaging them wrapped around my cock, slowly taking all of me. That pretty little mouth quiet while I fuck her, shutting up her insecure words as I ram down her throat over and over.

I told her she's beautiful.

And that I bet she has a sexy body under those layers.

That I dream about how she'd taste….

That I see her…

I'm out of my goddamn mind.

Still, it's her I see as I jerk myself faster, imagining she's sitting on me, my face buried in her tits as I suck on her nipples. Oh, I'd devour her if she'd let me. I'd make sure she remembered my name, and not just because it's on my cut, or because I barely wear any clothes, but because I wanna make her scream. I like the fact that she noticed.

When her hands touched my body, something happened to me. I didn't just have a wood the size of Brazil, I felt my heart literally skip a beat.

It's because she's not a woman I usually go for, I decide. She's not my type at all, which makes it a challenge…that's all it is.

I'm not growing feelings or some dumb shit like that.

I just need to fuck her, get it out of my system, prove to myself that that's all this is.

She's innocent, and the devil in me wants to taint her. Mark her. Make her mine.

It has nothing to do with anything other than the fact that I can't have her.

I imagine flipping her over, taking her from behind as she holds on to my headboard and sticks that beautiful booty out, slapping her ass cheeks I pump into her, listening as she wails…gripping her waist as I ram in and out…and I come all over myself, spurting hot cum all over my stomach.

Holy shit, that was intense. I'm dizzy as I let go of myself, tipping my head back until it hits the headboard. I came with thunder, imagining my baby doll and all the things I could do to her.

I reach for the tissues on the side table and wipe myself clean, shaking my head.

This won't do.

I could've just grabbed a sweet butt and nailed her, still imagining my baby girl, but since it's eleven o'clock in the morning and most of the chicks are asleep in one of the other brothers' beds, it wasn't really an option.

Like a little fucking errand boy, I took her order to her office, afraid she'd get in trouble for leaving without it, and that's when I learned where she works.

Now I can spy on her whenever I want.

I asked around; she's interning at the real estate office, and lives a few blocks from the clubhouse. Convenient.

She's left high school so she has to be eighteen, thank fuck, but the only thing that worries me now is when I'm gonna see her again.

I have to see her soon.

Someone bangs on my door. I quickly pull the duvet over my lap in case they barge in without being asked, my dick still hanging out from my jerk off session.

"Hutch, you in there?" Harlem yells through the door.

"Fuck off!" I yell back. "Busy in here."

"Need you downstairs in five. Pussy can wait."

Huh. If only.

I don't argue. If Harlem needs something, then that's what I'm here for.

I run a hand through my hair, needing a nap after what I just did to myself, but I get up anyway. Shucking into my jeans, I zip them up, pull on my cut, and tie my hair back into a small ponytail.

When I make my way downstairs, Grim is also waiting with Harlem.

I give them a chin lift. "What's up?"

"Scar thought it might be fun to take you along with us to see a client who hasn't paid up," Harlem explains.

My eyes light up. This is good; I'm gaining trust within the ranks. I've never been on a job where I tag along like this before.

"Sounds good."

"The guy's new in town, seems like he doesn't really understand how things work around here," Grim goes on. "So what better way to welcome him to Bracken Ridge, right?"

I smile. "Great, where to?"

Harlem reels off the address.

It doesn't take long to get there.

Nestled between two other businesses, the hardware

store has recently changed hands, that much we know. But it also seems that the old owners didn't pass the message that we require their loyalty. I mean, it is optional, but things can get very tricky if you're not with us. If you're not with us, then, yeah, you're against us.

Usually, an intimidation tactic like this is all we really need to reiterate what needs to happen. Haven't had anyone say no yet…

We enter the shop as the doorbell jingles and the man behind the counter looks up. He immediately puts his newspaper down and then his hands go to his hips.

"Are you John Mason?" Grim asks.

The man nods.

"The new owner?" he clarifies.

"What is this about?"

We flank him as I look around the front of the store, picking up objects here and there as he watches each of us in turn.

"A birdie told us that you're refusing to cooperate," Harlem begins. "And when that happens, we pay a little visit, to smooth everything out."

Grim spins the baseball bat in his hand. "Nice shop you have here."

"I'll call the police," John says, turning toward the phone, but Grim places his bat over the top of it.

"I wouldn't do that if I were you, and anyway, the

pigs in this town don't give a shit about you. They're in our pockets too." Grim smiles. "That's the beauty of small towns."

"You can't do this!" John spits angrily. "I won't pay money for…"

Grim swings the bat down on the telephone, smashing it to pieces. "You were saying?"

John's eyes go wide, then wisely, he keeps his mouth closed.

"This is how it's going to work," Grim carries on. "You're going to keep up the payments to the club and we won't be needing to come back and rearrange things. It looks like this store could do with a spring clean."

I snort.

Harlem smiles a rare smile. I think he's hoping he might get to crack John's head on the counter before we leave. Violence always seems to make him the happiest.

"I…I don't have that kind of money…" he stammers. "I just spent everything on buying the business…if I were to…"

"Excuses, excuses," I put in. "John, we're here to do you a favor. Don't make us regret it. This is a very small town and people need to rally together. Who knows what unfortunate things could happen to this shop if you choose to 'go it alone.' It would be such a damn shame to see this place go up in flames."

It's a low move, but I have to prove to my brothers that

I have the knack for it. Even if it bugs me that I have to threaten innocent people.

Beads of sweat form on my forehead.

"That it would." Grim points the bat at me, then moves it so it sits at John's chin, tapping it a few times. "We also wouldn't wanna fuck up this face for all the nice customers, would we?"

"You people!" he cries. "Daylight robbery is what this is, you can't do this!"

Grim grabs him by the head and shoves him down on the counter as he cries out.

I look away.

I don't like this. I know we all have the ability when it comes to self-defense, or sorting shit out when someone has done the club wrong, but this man is innocent.

And I can't help but feel a little guilty.

If he knows what's good for him, he'll pay the money and shut up.

"Now, repeat after me…you won't need to come back here again because I've learned my lesson."

He squirms and cries out as Grim holds him down so his cheek pushes up against the wood.

"I…I've…no, I…"

Grim pushes him harder. "You're only making this harder on yourself, and your family, you have a daughter, right?"

His eyes go wide.

We're not really gonna do anything…I don't think. It's just a tactic.

"Leave my daughter out of this!"

"Well, just remember that every time you think about not paying, John, that we can come back anytime and take what we want. Your daughter included."

I swallow hard, cracking my neck from side to side.

I didn't agree to this. To threatening innocent people and their families…

All the while, I keep up the pretense because I know Harlem is watching me. Like a damn hawk.

"I…said…okay!"

"A little louder, John," I pipe up, closing my eyes with my back to them. "For those in the back."

"I said I'll do it!" he bellows.

Grim lets him go. "Good. See how easy that was? Not hard at all, was it?"

Grim dusts himself off, giving Harlem a chin lift.

"Now you owe us for last week and two weeks up front," Harlem says, looking down at the petrified man.

He fumbles and makes his way to the till, opening it and taking out the cash.

Harlem tucks it into his pocket. "Now, that's as easy as it can be from now on. We won't need to have this discussion again, will we?"

John shakes his head. It's time to go before anyone else comes in.

I glance outside and see someone approach, then whistle to the boys.

"We got company."

"Remember what we said," Grim says, waving the baseball bat at John as we take our leave. He swipes all the things off the counter, and they clatter to the floor as I open the door, my eyes meeting with Kirsty's as she passes me and goes into the shop. Her head turns and so does mine.

Fuck.

This isn't what I wanted.

Grim gives her a once-over as the door closes behind her. The last thing I hear is her shrieking, "Dad! Oh no, what happened? What did they do to you?"

I stand below Kirsty's parents' house, throwing gravel at her window.

I couldn't turn around after we left her dad's shop. I don't want the brothers knowing that I know her, but I need to explain.

I wait a few moments, but when she doesn't appear at the window, I bend and grab another handful, then throw them against the pane.

Finally, the upstairs light goes on and she comes to the window. Looking down at the ground, she yanks the window up angrily. "What?" she spits.

"Can I come up?"

"No! Go away!" she whisper-shouts. "I don't want to see you ever again!"

"I need to explain!"

"You're going to wake my parents up, go away!"

"I'm comin' up!" I whisper-shout back, reaching up to the tree next to me as I swing a leg over.

"What?" she cries as I begin my ascent. "You can't come up here!"

Like fuck I can't.

"I need to talk to you," I mutter, doubting she can even hear me.

In an attempt to shove the window back down, it jams, and I use that valuable time to latch onto the drainpipe and climb up the side of the house faster, hoping like fuck I don't fall.

When I reach her, she's still trying to jimmy the widow down.

"What are you doing here?" she stammers, her face hot and flushed.

"I told you, I need to talk."

"I don't want to talk to you!"

"I'm comin' in," I tell her as her frantic eyes meet mine.

"You are not, Richie Hutchison. I hate you!"

I roll my eyes. "You know if I fall and die, those will be the last words I ever hear."

She shakes her head as I jump from the tree to the window ledge and somehow make it, my body flush up against the house as she frantically looks behind her.

"Shhh! If my parents wake up, we're both dead."

I push up onto my hands as she tries to let the window up to let me through and, eventually, it gives way and I slide in onto the floor, unceremoniously knocking over her plush toys on the window seat below.

"You can't be in here!" she goes on, like she didn't just help me through the window.

"Well," I say, standing, brushing the dirt and leaves from me. "It seems that I can and I did, and you won't talk to me, so I had no other choice."

"Yes, you did have a choice, Richie, the same choice you made to threaten my father because he won't do what you want him to do!"

"It's not me that wants it, baby girl, it's the club. There's a difference."

She shakes her head. "No, that's just an excuse, you're…you're…thugs!"

I grin, moving toward her as she takes a step back. "You don't mean that."

"I'm warning you!"

I hold my hands in front of me, palms facing her. "I'm not going to hurt you."

She snorts. "Just like you didn't hurt my dad?"

"Technically, that wasn't me, it was Grim. He was a little outta line."

"A little?" She pushes me in the chest. "Go away!"

"Just let me talk, please, Kirsty…"

She shakes her head. "I don't want you to be here."

Right, like I believe that for a single second.

"Just give me one minute to explain. Can you do that for me?"

She gives me a look that could cut glass, and I try not to grin.

Oh, I like this Kirsty. She has a fiery side.

"Please?" I beg, folding my hands together like I'm praying.

She huffs, folding her arms over her ample chest, which I've just noticed as she's wearing pajamas and they cling to her body. "You have thirty seconds, Richie Hutchinson, and if you don't get your point across by then, I'm screaming." She wags a finger in my face. "And believe me, there isn't a person in Bracken Ridge that won't hear me."

There's my girl.

I step toward her and say, "You're so much cuter when you're mad."

BRACKEN RIDGE
REBELS
ARIZONA
M · C

CHAPTER 5

HABSTY

You're so much cuter when you're mad?

What the hell?

I shake my head. "You're disgusting, do you know that? Threatening innocent people into paying you. For a second there, I thought you were actually a half-decent person, but now I think you're just a big jerk!"

I can't help it, I'm furious.

I saw what they did to my dad and to his shop, and I want to punch him in the face for it.

I don't even know why I let him up here, maybe so I could just go ahead and kick him out again. Get the upper hand, even though I know that's fruitless. He's a biker.

"Why was I only a half-decent person?" he queries, probably guessing I'm about to throw something at his head.

I step back as he takes a step toward me.

"Because you did that thing where you brought my coffee order to the office so I didn't get in trouble, which was a nice thing to do…but that's not the point…" Why am

I such a loser?

A smile spreads across his face. "You like me."

"Get over yourself."

"Don't deny it."

"I am denying it, you're disgusting. You and your stupid club!"

"Then why am I here?"

Good question. Why indeed?

"Because I wanted to tell you to your face that you're a jerk and I hate you."

I stare at him in the face as he doesn't even attempt to back off.

Strangely, I'm not afraid of him. And that is very, very dumb.

I should be. I should run a mile. After what he and his buddies did to my dad's shop, as well as assaulting and terrorizing him.

"You don't hate me, Kirsty," he says in that smooth voice of his. "You wish you did, though."

I shake my head. "People like you are what's wrong with the world."

His eyebrows raise in question. "Is that right?"

"Yes! You can't make a decent living on your own merits or by working hard. Instead you have to terrorize innocent people into giving you money for just existing. Tell me, Richie, how do you sleep at night?"

Maybe I've stepped over the line, but I don't care. He can go to hell.

"It's not like that," he begins, his voice softer as I try not to let the pounding of my heart take over.

I've never had a boy in my room before, not even close.

Again, I wonder why he's even here. Why does he care what I think?

It's like he really does want to explain, but that makes no sense. He's clearly someone with no ethics or morals.

"Really? So what is it like?" I fire back. "Because I'd love to know."

"This is how biker clubs run," he begins. "It's how it's always been. We don't want to start or stir up trouble, we want to keep the peace."

"Ha!" I snort. "By threatening people into paying you 'protection money?' What kind of people are you?"

He shrugs. "You're right."

Huh?

I narrow my eyes. "Now you're just going to agree with me? Make up your mind."

"Oh, I have made up my mind." His eyes skim down my body in a way that makes my skin tingle.

I'm only wearing pajamas, something only my parents have ever seen me in.

I swallow hard.

"You need to go." Even my own voice doesn't sound

convincing.

"Fine, but you said you'd hear me out."

"No, I said you had thirty seconds, and your time is up."

His eyes meet mine again. "Am I forgiven?"

I shake my head. "For hurting my dad? No."

"What about for being a jerk?"

I shake my head again.

Glancing at his chest as he towers over me, I feel that burn again, the one between my legs. The one that tells me he's all wrong for me, but I don't care.

I want to slap myself for being so dumb.

He doesn't care; the only person Richie Hutchison cares about is himself.

But his body…he wears a tight shirt, and every single fiber clings to him, showing the outline of his perfectly sculpted muscles. My eyes dip lower, to his belt buckle, then to the bulge at the front of his jeans. Holy hell.

"Baby girl?" he whispers as I snap my head back up. "Do you forgive me for being a jerk?"

I shake my head again.

"No?" he goes on. "Then why does your skin go red every time I'm near you? Why does your bottom lip tremble whenever I'm close?"

"It doesn't!"

He pushes my hair back from my shoulder, but doesn't touch me. "Yes, it does. Your nipples…why do they pucker when I tell you you're beautiful and I want to taste you?"

I reach out to slap him, but he catches my hand mid-swing. "I hate you!"

"No, baby, you don't, the reality is, you want me as much as I want you, don't you?" He holds on to my wrist as I try to wriggle free. Giving up, he lets me go.

"No! I don't. I want you to leave…" Even to me it doesn't sound true.

"You're wet, Kirsty. Aren't you, baby girl? You want me to relieve the ache between your legs."

I open my mouth, then close it again. Is that an option? No! Stop it! Be strong. You don't need him.

"Has anyone ever touched you there?" He looks down toward my mid-section, his eyes dipping lower.

"That's none of your business!" I know my voice is coming out strained and whiny, but it's not my fault. He's getting me all hot and bothered, and I don't want this.

I don't…I do… If only he hadn't come into my dad's store and done that. How could anyone do such a thing?

"I wanna make it my business. All my business."

He's so goddamn close, but he refuses to touch me, and I think that's why he's doing it. To torture me some more.

"Is that honestly why you came here?" I blurt out. "To mock me?"

He frowns. "Mock you?"

"Yes!" I shove him in the chest. "Mock me! Do you get

some sick pleasure in doing that? In making me feel like a complete idiot? Because trust me, pal, I get enough of that from everyone else around me because I don't fit into the box or mold they want me to. Every day I hear and see it, and the last thing I need is you up here, in my bedroom, making me feel like shit as well, got it?" Now he's making me curse.

He shakes his head, his hands going to his hips, where they stay. "I'm not mocking you, baby girl. I would never do that. Anyone who did that to you is a fucking dick."

"Then why?" I poke him in the chest. "Why do you keep saying those things?"

He reaches for me once more, and damn it, I let him touch me. He cups one side of my face, his hand calloused but warm, and it sends shock waves right through me.

"Because I meant what I said; you're beautiful…there's something about you. I don't know what it is. I wish I knew; that's the truth."

He seems so sincere. But how could he be?

I'm nobody. Nothing.

Fat. Frumpy. Disgusting.

That's how I've been made to feel my whole life since I hit puberty. But Hutch…he doesn't look at me like that. He looks at me like I'm a woman. And dammit if I'm not falling for it, even if I do still want to slap him after what they did to my dad in his store.

"I'm nothing," I whisper, echoing my own thoughts. "I'm nobody."

His eyes grow fierce. "Did somebody tell you that? Because if they did…I'll fucking end them."

I bite down on my lip as his forehead touches mine, unable to answer.

"When you bite down like that…baby girl, it makes me want to be a very bad man."

His chest touches mine as he crowds me farther, his body pressing into me, and I feel the bulge in his jeans press into my core. He's rock hard.

"Richie…" I whisper.

"Hutch, baby girl," he replies. "You can call me Richie when I make you come."

I clench my core as his words hit me like a ton of bricks. I practically come undone on the spot, and I hate myself for it.

"You're not a good person," I whisper as he moves his head. His lips skim my neck, but he doesn't kiss me. He teases me. Something he's becoming very, very good at.

My hands move to clutch his forearms. I don't know if it's to stop or encourage him. The jury's still out on that.

"I'm not a bad one, either, not when you get to know me."

My nipples peak, needing attention, and he moves his mouth closer to my ear. "I asked you a question earlier about if anyone has touched you."

I swallow hard.

"Has anyone, Kirsty?"

"No," I whisper.

He grunts his approval. "What about here?" He cups one of my breasts, and I jerk in response.

I shake my head.

His thumb moves to my lips, swiping across the bottom one as I squirm beneath his touch, my panties soaked. "Here?"

I shake my head.

"Have you ever been kissed?"

I shake my head.

He shakes his in dismay. "You're fuckin' kiddin' me?"

"Boys aren't into me." I can barely get the words out. "I'm not…their idea of what's attractive."

"Boys might not be, but I'm a man, Kirsty." He grabs one hand and moves it swiftly to cup the bulge in his jeans. "Do you feel that, baby girl? Does that feel like I'm not into you?"

My eyes go wide as my heart races so fast, I'm sure it's going to explode. He holds the palm of my hand there as I try not to burn up.

It's so stiff. He moves his hand with mine, showing me his length, letting me feel all of him. I don't know a lot about penises, but his feels damn huge..

My mouth forms an 'O' as he makes noises while continuing to rub himself with my hand.

"Does that feel like I'm playin' with you? Mocking you? Nope, I can't fake that." His voice is coarse and so damn sexy. "I want to fuck you, Kirsty. Is that direct enough for you?"

My eyes go wide as they meet his. I begin to tremble.

"Here? Like in my parents' house?"

He chuckles. "No, baby girl, not here."

"I…I uh…I never…"

He swipes his thumb over my lower lip again. "You're still a virgin, right?"

My cheeks burn. "Y…yes."

I know I'm just a conquest to him, that I won't matter once it's over with, but at this point, I have to ask myself if I even care.

Richie is the sexiest, hottest guy I've ever laid eyes on…why did he have to hurt my dad? It clawed at me, making me feel guilt ridden and like I'm a bad daughter.

"Do you like how that feels, Kirsty?"

I love how he says my name like that. I'm delirious.

Still rubbing him, I nod.

"How does it feel?"

I swallow hard. "Huge."

He smiles, touching my chin once more and bringing my head up to look at him. "Are you eighteen?"

"Yes, I'll be nineteen in a few months."

He looks relieved. "I want to kiss you."

"Uh…" I panic. I want to, but he's…he's everywhere.

"Is that a yes?"

I bite my lip but manage a nod. I wish I could stop my body responding, but it seems that Hutch owns all my responses now as well as my dignity, or what's left of it.

He moves his head down. "Good girl." He presses his lips to mine suddenly, and I make a sound I've never made before. His lips are surprisingly soft, as is the scruff around his face. One of his hands cups my cheek, the other still holds my hand over his dick, and it seems to be getting harder…if that is at all possible.

I moan softly when his tongue gently touches mine, clutching my free hand into his shirt, bringing him closer.

It's my first kiss.

And it's freaking perfect.

When he pulls back, we're both panting, and my body is on fire.

"Better stop rubbing me, baby girl." His voice is barely audible. "Or I'll come in my pants."

I bite my lip as he frees it with his thumb and moves his mouth back over mine, sucking on my bottom lip as I throw my arms around his neck. Pushing his hardness into my center, I feel dizzy. He walks me back toward my bed, but doesn't lay me down. Instead, he moves me to the side table, where he sits my ass down, shoving my book to one side.

"Not gonna fuck you here, under your parents' roof," he mutters, his eyes blazing as I pant, looking up at him, knowing my face is on fire. "But I do wanna claim your first orgasm."

My eyes go wide. He comes toward me, standing in between my legs, the huge bulge in his jeans front and center as he reaches down to cup my breast. Unbuttoning the top button of my flannel top, he groans when he pulls it to one side, my breast popping out.

"Fuckin' beautiful."

Before I can protest, he moves his mouth down and over my nipple as I squirm around, my hands reaching into his hair as he sucks and plays with it. His fingers deftly unbutton the rest of my top as he shoves the shirt off my shoulders and moves his mouth to my other eagerly awaiting nipple. He's greedy, taking his time.

Shifting his body even closer, he moves so his knee is between my legs and I'm pushed up against it.

The sensation is…like nothing else…

"Richie!" I cry, my mouth at his shoulder as he sucks, plucks, and licks my nipples, making them so hard, I could scream the house down.

"That's it, baby." He cups my mound through my pj pants as I almost combust. "I wanna taste you so badly."

His dirty words just about send me into oblivion.

Looking up at me, I squeeze my eyes shut as his eyes tell me how much he wants me. It's a new sensation; I see myself in his eyes and I realize I am beautiful.

I am everything, not nothing.

I may hate that it's taken this man to make me realize it, and I don't like it one bit, but for now, I want to enjoy what he's doing. I can always go back to hating him later…

"Touch me," I beg. "Touch me there."

I hold his hand at the apex of my thighs as he grunts, his mouth kissing my breasts all over as he mutters into my skin. His hand slides under the elastic of my pj pants and past my panties, which are soaked.

"Fuck," he mutters when he feels how wet I am. "Fuck, fuck, fuck."

He closes his eyes, stopping his ministrations for a moment as I look down at him.

My tits are hanging out and he rests his head on them, squeezing his eyes shut like he's praying.

"Richie?" I whisper. "Are you okay?"

His hand is still in my pants, my slickness coating his fingers as his eyes open.

"I want you so bad," he tells me. "So bad, baby girl. Like nothin' else. I'm so hard…"

I want him too. But I can't do this in my parents' house…can I?

I wait. Hoping. Hoping he'll at least give me what I want the most…my first orgasm.

I'm unashamed at this point in time, and needy.

I'm needy for him.

This badass biker who just broke into my house. The man who was there when my father was assaulted by his club brothers.

I can't get enough of Richie Hutchison.

BRACKEN RIDGE
REBELS
ARIZONA
M · C

CHAPTER 6

HUTCH

"Please," she begs me. "Richie, don't stop."

It's like music to my ears.

I don't want to stop, that's the problem. And I can't take her here.

Not like this.

As much as my dick is telling me I want to, and as much as she's telling me she wants to. I shake myself out of the fog.

Her hands on me…her tits…they're so big and beautiful. Perfectly formed, I could feast on them for the rest of eternity. As I reveal more of her skin, I'm wondering why she has some kind of body image problem. I can't wrap my head around it. She's fuckin' gorgeous.

Curvy, yes. Fat, no. I like a woman with meat on her bones. I like a round stomach, full tits, and a plump ass. I like everything Kirsty Mason has to offer. And I know that if I rush this and take her virginity now, I'll only regret not taking my time once it's over.

Lord knows, I want to.

I want to take it hard and fast. Claiming her. Making her mine.

Knowing I'm gonna be the first one does things to me. It makes me giddy like a goddamn schoolboy.

And when she begs me…I want to fucking die.

I gather myself, my hand in her panties, covered in her juices. I want to bury my head between her legs, eat her out until she's screaming my name, lapping her up until she can't bear it anymore and we fuck for the first time. But I can't do any of that here.

I've gotta plan this right. I've got to do it properly, so it's good for her.

I'm not like other assholes. I like her. I really fuckin' like her. And something inside me cares about disappointing her, which is stupid. I don't care about chicks like this. I don't usually give a shit about their feelings or if it's good for them, too. We both get off and that's normally good enough. But with Kirsty, I want it all.

I'm her first kiss. The first to finger her. The first to give her an orgasm, and I'll be the first to pop that sweet cherry. I can't help but gloat just a little.

"You're so wet," I growl. "Hold your titties up to my mouth. Let me tease them."

She does as I say, cupping herself as I latch onto one nipple, suckling one then the other. My fingers start to play with her pussy as she groans low, her noises making me leak into my pants. There's no room for what I have going on down there, but I have to make do. I know I'm probably not gonna get off tonight, but for some reason, this has become more about her than it is about me.

And I like that.

I tap my fingers on her pussy, moving them along the seam and up to her clit. When I get there, I start to rub her clit around and around as her panting becomes louder.

I don't even care. Her dad can fuckin' shoot me at this point. I want her orgasm and I want to see her come.

Looking up, her eyes meet mine as I move my mouth to her other peak and suckle as she pushes her chest out, trying to get more of her into my mouth.

"Oh, oh," she starts.

Not changing the pace, not penetrating her hole, I just watch her unravel.

"Yes!" she cries as I leave her tits and cover my mouth with hers as she starts to shake.

My tongue in her mouth, she detonates all over my fingers as I drown out her moans and ride her through her pleasure.

When she's done, I know I'm not. I need to finger her tight hole. I want to savor this for later, when I'm choking my cock with my own hand.

Her eyes are still closed when I move my fingers down,

but they open as I move the tip of my finger inside. Her eyes meet mine. She's flushed beautifully, her cheeks stained red and her eyes slightly out of focus.

"How did I do?" I whisper.

"Perfect," she gasps.

"Gonna put my finger a little deeper," I grunt. "Need to feel how tight you are."

She doesn't stop me, and I chuckle as I slide my finger all the way in, pulling another groan from her chest. Her hands still cup her tits as I move my other hand to one breast and knead it in my roughened palm.

"That feels good, so good."

"Imagine my dick inside," I whisper. "Imagine me sliding in and out of you, my fat cock taking your pussy, Kirsty, over and over, until you scream my name like I'm a fuckin' curse."

"I want that."

She's so slick as I continue to finger her. I could slide right in there. It'd still be tight. I'm big. And she's not. But still, it'd be so fucking perfect....

I want to put another finger inside, and when I do, she arches her back and starts to move her hips. Holy shit.

"That's it, baby." I still haven't seen her pussy, and if I do, I might actually just rip her pants down and take her hard and fast like I want to. "You look so good riding my hand, baby girl."

She wraps her arms around me as I nuzzle into her neck, my fingers working in and out of her slowly, letting her feel every sensation.

When my thumb grazes her clit, she squeezes my goddamn fingers, and I cover her mouth again with mine, scared I'll wake her parents if she's too loud.

The sound. The goddamn sound she makes. I'm leaking bad, but I don't care.

With her lips pressed against mine, something entirely new moves through me. A new sensation I've never felt before.

I'm protective of her.

I don't understand it.

"Richie," she tries to garble as I grin against her, riding out her orgasm again. Smug that I gave her two. She's panting when we're done, her chest rising and falling fast. Her lips swollen from our kisses, my hand still in her pants as we hear a noise.

Her eyes going wide. She grabs onto her shirt and quickly starts to button it up as I remove my hand, wiping it on the back of my jeans.

"You have to go," she whispers, grabbing me by the hem of my shirt.

"So soon?" I mock, adjusting my dick because I'm so hard it's ridiculous.

"You'll have to go out the way you came in," she says

gravely, looking out the window and wincing. "Sorry."

I pull her into my arms, kissing her again as she pushes against me. "You'll be sorry the next time I get you alone." I cup her sex. "I want this, baby girl."

"Richie, you have to go! That's probably my parents!"

I grin, though I don't care about getting caught by them. I only care that she'll be in trouble.

Ducking out the window, I give her a wink. "Keep your window closed at night. You don't know what kind of misfits are lurking around."

She shakes her head, but I see the humor in her eyes.

I hang onto the tree, escaping death just barely, as I make my way down. Once at the bottom and my feet hit the ground, I look up. She hangs out of the window.

"I'll be back, Kirsty!" I cup my mouth as I try not to yell that to the whole neighborhood.

"Go!" She shoos me away like a hen as I take off running. Hoping that she isn't sprung.

I doubt her parents would think anything untoward was going on in their innocent little girl's room. She's been tainted now, though.

I've had a taste and I want more.

Bringing my fingers up to my nose, I inhale her scent. Shit. I suck my fingers into my mouth, wishing I had one more second to make her feel good.

But I will.

She'll be beneath me soon.

And hell hath no fury like a man who wants what he wants.

And I'm gonna get it.

Kirsty Mason is mine, no matter what she says.

I get back to the clubhouse and I'm frustrated beyond belief.

It's Friday, so everyone is drinking and there's loud music blasting from the jukebox.

The boys usually play pool, drink to excess, and fuck wherever the panties land.

Usually, it's anywhere but in private.

As soon as I walk in the door, heads turn my way.

It's been a productive day, even if I did almost fuck things up with Kirsty's dad.

I still feel very bad about that and what she said has been gnawing at me.

Why I give a fuck, I don't know, but when a sweet butt's hands glide around my waist, reaching to squeeze my ass, I take a deep breath.

I don't know what the fuck is wrong with me. I need to get off. I want to get off.

And I could. Yet, all I can think about is getting off with

no one but Kirsty.

Her words about her basically not being good enough echo in my ears and I don't understand a damn thing. It's like I'm tuned into the right radio station but she's on static. I don't understand what she sees about herself that's ugly. Okay, maybe her clothes are a little dowdy, but that's probably because she wears excessively baggy outfits to cover up what she thinks is fat.

I think it's fucking glorious.

Thinking about her big tits and where I just had my hands makes me want to go running back to her house, fuck the rules, and finish the job.

Instead, I put an arm around Mindy and pull her closer. I don't want her, but I gotta make it seem like nothing's wrong.

I need a goddamn drink.

"How are you, Hutchy?" she purrs in my ear.

"Been better," I reply honestly as I make my way to the bar.

"Yeah? Can I help with that, baby?" She glances down my body, no doubt spotting the wood I'm sporting, and pinches my ass even harder.

"You can help by gettin' me a drink, sugar lips."

She pouts, but goes off and does as she's told. I sit, running a hand through my hair as I sigh loudly.

"Tough night?" Harlem gives me a chin lift.

"You could say that."

"Think you learned a thing or two today?"

I don't want to think about what we put Kirsty's dad through, to be quite honest, but I play the game.

"Don't fuck with the Bracken Ridge Demons?"

He grunts a laugh into his beer. "You sure you got the chops for this?"

I frown. Does he think I don't? This isn't good. Harlem is the club's Enforcer. He demands respect just because of his position, and this could be a trick question. I saw how he was watching me, and make no mistake, he will report everything back to Scar.

"I'm more than sure. Fucker deserved it."

He grunts again, then he says, "Some brothers wouldn't be able to handle the shit that we do, especially when it's aimed at innocent people."

Where is he going with this? And why is he on the 'innocent people' bandwagon? None of the brothers see locals or anyone around here as being innocent.

"Not me," I say. "I'm up for anything."

"Even when it counts?"

"Especially then."

"Hmm."

I turn to him. "You think I don't?"

"Didn't say that."

"Then what is it?"

"My dad used to run a hardware store."

"So?"

"So, it sucks to be the little guy."

My frown deepens. What the fuck is he talking about? This is what we do.

I know there's been a lot of friction in the club between Scar and just about everybody, but the Enforcer saying these things? It makes me wonder if there is an underlying problem going on that none of us except committee members are aware of.

"It's the nature of the business," I say, when I can't think of anything else. Maybe Scar's put him up to this, to try to stir some emotion in me so I'll be ridiculed for being soft, unable to do the hard things the club wants me to do. Tests like this don't happen all the time, but they do happen.

Deep down, I know it's wrong. All of it.

And I wish I could get Kirsty's words out of my head, but as much as I try, I can't.

She called us a bunch of thugs.

I sit with that for a moment, but it feels off. I don't like her thinking bad about me and I've no idea why I care.

I don't even wait for Mindy to come back with my drink.

I push off the bar.

"Hey, where you goin'?" Harlem calls after me.

"Bed," I call back over my shoulder.

I can't sit here any longer with my head pounding like it is.

This wasn't supposed to happen.

I don't even know her. Yet, even when my head hits the pillow as I go to bed alone, hers is the face I see.

And there isn't a goddamn thing I can do about it.

BRACKEN RIDGE
REBELS
ARIZONA
M.C.

CHAPTER 7

KIRSTY

A week goes by, and I've stayed away from the coffee shop.

I've heard a motorcycle pass by the office daily, and by my house. I know it's him.

One time, I looked out, and I saw him looking up at my window.

With my heart palpitating like a runaway freight train, I couldn't bring myself to let him see me.

Do I regret it? No.

Would I do it again? I don't know. I mean, I want to do so much more, but I can't get over how violent this motorcycle club is. Why does it have to be this way? Why do they hurt innocent people and threaten them if they don't comply?

And…is Hutch a violent person, I just haven't been around him long enough to know that?

I think about the times I've been around him, and I've yet to feel afraid of him.

He does intimidate me, but not in a scary way. No, in a way that I've never been touched or kissed by a man like him before, and I'm so inexperienced that I don't know if what I did was okay or if he enjoyed it. I mean, he seemed to, but he left with an extremely large bulge in his pants and he didn't get off. Not that I was going to let him have sex with me in my bedroom with my parents next door. I close my eyes, thinking about how he felt under my palm. A noise leaves my throat as I remember how thick he was. How hard. He got me so wet that I was embarrassed, not that he seemed to mind.

All the while, I know it's wrong to fantasize about him.

I can't even imagine what my parents would do if they found out.

We've finally settled here, and with my dad buying the hardware store, things are finally starting to feel good. And now this.

I know I need to stay away from him.

But that all changes when my mom and I are shopping the next day.

As usual, she's on her own little warpath about how my life should be run. Not for the first time, I think about moving out, but I'd have to get a better paying job, one that pays more than what I'm getting at the real estate office. It barely covers my tuition.

"...for Thanksgiving, it'll be nice to have your sister

home for the holiday."

I internally groan. No, it won't. I often wonder if me and my sister are even from the same family and one of us isn't secretly adopted.

"Mmhmm." It's really all I can manage.

"Stand up straight, Kirsty," Mom chastises. "Is it any wonder you didn't make the cheerleading squad with posture like that."

Yeah. I loved cheerleading, then puberty hit, and I gained weight. She knows this.

She knows how triggering my weight is for me.

3. 2. 1…

"You know, it wouldn't hurt you to try that new diet Darlene was talking about. It might help."

I keep quiet. The watercress soup diet? Right, like that sounds delicious.

Little does Mom know, I have lost five pounds, not that anyone would know because I still cover myself.

Why do you wear these big, baggy sweaters? It's almost eighty degrees outside. Hutch's voice echoes in my head.

The reason I asked is because I think you're the most beautiful woman I've ever seen with the prettiest eyes and mouth…I like your attitude. It's turnin' a little on the snarky side right now, but I can overlook that…I bet you have a sexy body under all those layers, you just don't know how to show it off properly…

Trust me, I've never felt sexy ever in my life nor have I been called it, which is why I got so mad at Hutch when he said it, thinking he was making fun of me. The last thing I need in my life is more ridicule.

After he said those things, I took a good, long look in the mirror, something I usually try to avoid, and a strange thing happened…I saw myself differently. For the very first time, I didn't hate what I saw.

Nothing has really changed since the last time I looked, except maybe the five pounds I've lost. I've been trying to exercise more and watch what I eat. I'm not an unhealthy person; in fact, some of the anxiety medication I've been taking made me gain weight, but I'm slowly weening myself off them, and I'm starting to feel good again.

I even tried on a pair of fitted jeans today, and I felt good. They're a snug fit, but I didn't think I looked like a dump truck.

Have I been seeing myself through other people's eyes, like my mom's, instead of my own?
Have I been too hard on myself?

And more importantly, why did it take Hutch telling me these things to make me realize? Should I be mad at him, or thank him? I don't feel like I need a man's approval, not that it doesn't feel good, but I've never been that type of woman.

I never want to have the kind of relationship like my parents have; a business transaction. There's very little love or joy between them and I think that's extremely sad.

I realize my mom's looking at me sternly.

"Sorry?" I say, realizing I totally missed whatever she's been saying.

"Your weight, Kirsty. The watercress soup diet might help."

I sigh. "Mom, can't you just give it a rest for five minutes? We're shopping…people can hear." I lower my voice at that last part.

She shakes her head. "I'm only trying to help. This is your father's fault. I should never have let you leave gymnastics so early."

"You can't beat puberty, Mom," I say insolently. "I'm sorry I'm not anything like Darlene, but I'm actually pretty happy with how I look." I'm not entirely, but for some reason, it shoots out of my mouth before I can stop it.

She stops the cart and stares at me. "Kirsty? What did you just say to me?"

Nothing, Mom, only eighteen years of being told I'm not good enough.

"I'm sorry I'm not the daughter you hoped I'd be."

Her eyes go wide. "What's gotten into you?" she snarls, looking around quickly. "I didn't raise you to talk back like this. All I'm trying to do is help you…"

"What if I don't want your help?" I fire back. "What if I'm tired of hearing that I'm not good enough? Too fat.

Too frumpy. Too this, too that… What if I'm actually okay in my own skin? Why do I always have to justify myself in your eyes?"

Her face turns a shade of red I've never seen before. "We will discuss this when we get home."

I shake my head, backing away. Suddenly, I want to be free. Free of it all, over this chokehold she has over me and how she always puts me down. Every single conversation we have is about how I look, why I don't go to college, like Darlene, how I should dress, how I should talk, what I should do with my life…I can't deal with it anymore.

I had no idea I'd wake up today and it would be a turning point for me, that I would finally lose it.

"No, Mom, we won't. I'm tired of you putting me down all the time. I don't want to be thin, I don't want to be pretty like Darlene, in fact, I don't want a damn thing from you!"

A moment passes where no words are exchanged. Then… "Don't you use the Lord's name in vain with me, missy!" She tries to grab my arm, but I'm too fast. "Wait till your father hears about this!"

I turn and run.

I don't know where I'm going or what I'm going to do, but I know I can't be within a ten-mile radius of her negativity right now.

I only stop running when I'm out of breath and my legs feel like jelly. I lean back against the wall and close my eyes, trying to get my breath back.

It's then I hear the loud noise of a motorcycle engine. I open my eyes, and sure enough, I see Hutch riding up the street, his eyes on me as he pulls up to the curb.

I stay where I am, pressed against the bricks, tears escaping as I try to hold them in.

He dismounts, leaving the beast running.

"Kirsty?" He frowns, looking down at me.

"Are you following me?" I fire at him, unsure why I'm mad at him.

"No, I saw you run out of the grocery store…is everything…"

"No, it's not okay." I nod to his bike. "I want to go for a ride with you."

His eyebrows shoot up in surprise. "Are you sure?" He wipes a stray tear away with his thumb. The gesture is so gentle and so unexpected, my bottom lip starts to tremble.

I nod. "Just tell me one thing."

He cups one side of my face, concern written all over his. "Of course."

"Are you just playing with me?"

His deep blue eyes stare right into mine, and I try not to shudder. The intensity…I've never felt anything like it. He cages me in, both hands resting beside my head against the wall. "No, Kirsty, I'm not. I don't know what this thing is between us; I don't even understand it, but there's something here. I can't stop thinking about you…"

Maybe I'm stupid. Maybe I'm naive. Maybe I'm gullible or all the above, but all I know right now is I want to be with him. On the back of his motorcycle, riding to anywhere that's far away from here. I need to clear my head.

"Let's go, then," I say, pushing him in the chest as I move forward. I grab his hand and tug him toward his waiting motorcycle. "I want to ride with you."

He adjusts our hands so they're linked, and I've never felt so much warmth in any single action before. It's like he has a spell on me that I can't shake. I don't want to shake it.

I want to bask in it.

I'm not ashamed that it feels good, maybe that's why I'm gravitating to him. I don't care. I don't want to overthink it, I just want to go.

We get to the bike, and he reaches for the helmet hanging from the handlebars. Before I can change my mind, he slides it down over my head, amusement playing on his lips.

Reaching toward me, he gives me a quick peck on the lips, turns and swings his leg over the beast, kicking up the stand, and then turns to pat the seat behind him. "Hop on, baby girl."

I don't hesitate. I climb on, holding on to him as I swing a leg over and wrap my arms around his waist.

He smells so good.

That same, musky, masculine scent that I swear I won't ever be able to forget. Everything about him is unforgettable.

He pats my leg. "You ready?"

I nod.

"Hold on tight, lean the same way I do when we go around corners, got me?"

"Yes," I say, feeling more exhilaration than I do fear.

He pats my hands as he checks his side mirror, then takes off from the curb with an almighty roar that could wake the dead.

People up the street turn and stare as we take off.

For the first time in a long time, I smile…this is what it feels like to be free.

Hutch takes the 101 so we ride out of town, along the almost deserted highway, and turns at the sign where it says: Shotgun Canyon.

I've not been up here since we moved. My parents aren't really campers or folk that should be out in the wilderness. I, on the other hand, love it.

The wind in your hair. The fresh air in your lungs. The smell and taste of the desert. It's like an elixir running through my veins as I hold tightly on to Hutch, feeling like I'm on a high I may never come down from.

Is this what it feels like to be happy?
I don't even care if it lasts. I'll remember today for the rest of my life.

Not just because I'm here, on a wild ride with the man I'm quickly falling for - very stupid - but because I finally had the gumption to stand up to my mom. And it's been a long time coming.

I don't even care what happens when I get home. I don't even want to go home; it's the furthest thing from my mind right now.

When we eventually stop, I'm so exhilarated, that the moment I slide off and Hutch takes the helmet from me, I fold into his arms and kiss him before he's even dislodged himself from the bike.

I swing my arms around his neck, pulling him closer, and the sweetest thing is…he reciprocates. His tongue finds mine as I hear a low growl escape him…I swear, every time I hear that noise, I want to combust. I want to be his everything. I want him to take me to the ends of the earth and never return. Not back to the sad, pathetic life I've been living.

I just want to live and breathe in this moment for a while longer…

When we pull back, we're both panting. He cups my

face, my arms still around his neck.

"Baby," he whispers, his lips still touching mine. "If you don't wanna lose your virginity up against a tree, I suggest we take a beat."

I giggle, pressing my lips against his again for a quick peck. "Thank you," I whisper.

He frowns. "What for?"

"For being you."

His lips curl up. "Nobody has ever said that to me before, baby girl…and I think I like it."

I pull my arms away, straightening myself as he dismounts.

"That was amazing," I say as he leans his ass against the side of his bike and beckons me with the crook of his finger.

"You liked it?"

I beam. "Can't you tell?"

I melt into his arms once more, his arms folding around my neck as mine slide around his waist. I stand between his legs, and it feels like the safest place in the world.

He kisses me on the forehead. "You wanna talk about it?"

I shake my head. "I don't want to sour the mood."

"You won't. Just know, if you want to, I'm a pretty good listener."

I snort. "That's rare for a man. You continue to surprise me at every turn."

"I'm glad about that, not the rare part, the part about me surprising you. I like it."

"I needed it. I love the feeling of being on the back with you, the wind in my hair, the breeze on my face, the smell of the desert."

"I like you being on the back," he says, his tone sincere. "I like everything about you, baby girl."

I look down momentarily, then back up at him. I want to tell him. I want to tell him everything.

But I'm afraid.

I've never been able to open up to anyone, until now. Until this very moment.

And I have him to thank for it.

BRACKEN RIDGE
REBELS
ARIZONA
M · C

CHAPTER 8

HUTCH

I stare down at this woman in wonder.

To say she's slowly snaring pieces of my heart is an understatement. For one, I didn't even know I had a heart until recently.

She brings out a side of me that I didn't know existed. I've always treated women with respect, even the sweet butts who act like prostitutes, and I've never struck a woman ever in my life - I never would - not after what my own piece of shit dad did to my mom, but I've also never cared. Not enough to get a permanent piece. Not enough to want to be with the same woman more than once, much less every night.

Kirsty has suddenly turned everything upside down. And I don't know why.

At first, I thought it was because I couldn't have her. She's too good for me; I'm fully aware of that, but she's also too smart and she sees right through me.

With her, there's a softness in me that wants to nurture her.

I care about what she thinks. I care about what she's doing. I care about what I can do to try to make her smile.

What in the actual fuck is happening to me, I don't know.

Normally, when women try to change me, or want to hang around and insert themselves into my life, I run a mile. I don't want it. As I've said many times, I don't believe in the sanctity of marriage or being with just one woman, the thought is unfathomable. Yet, when I think about being with another woman, I start to retreat. When I think about Kirsty with another man, I want to end him. Literally, end him.

I press my forehead against hers as we stand there, wrapped around one another.

Her eyes plead with me. I know something really bad must have happened to make her bolt like that, to make her cry. I don't like it when she cries. I never want to be the person that makes her shed tears. I learned that today.

She surprises me when she says, "I had a big fight with my mom."

I don't say anything, I just hold her.

"She started up again about me not being good enough and how I should try the watercress soup diet if I wanted to lose weight…" she trails off, her voice fading to a whisper. "And how my perfect sister is so much better than me. It's the same old story that I've been hearing my whole life."

I hate that her mom said those things and that's the reason

she fled. I don't understand why her mom doesn't see the beautiful, smart, amazing young woman she is. I'm dumbfounded.

"Baby, you know your mom's wrong. I know you don't believe this, but I never once thought you had a weight problem, not once. Do you hear me? I love your curves, you're beautiful. There is nothing about you I would want to change."

Her eyes stare up into mine, and I see the confusion. She's never been told before how beautiful she is. And that fucks with me big time. I don't get what other people aren't seeing, especially her own parents.

"And you're not just saying that?"

I kiss her lightly on the lips. "You felt my cock the other night." I glance down at my crotch. "And you can see now what you do to me. Does that look like I'm just sayin' it?"

I don't mention that it isn't just physical, that my heart races in my chest like I'm having a heart attack whenever I'm with her. That I can't stop thinking about her day and night. I don't want to sound like a pussy.

A small smile plays on her lips. "What are you doing to me?" she whispers.

I chuckle. "No, what are you doing to me?"

Her smile fades. "I just had enough, you know, of my mom putting me down. I finally flipped, right in the middle of the supermarket. It's like all the years of pent-up frustration and anxiety just all came bubbling to the surface, and then I couldn't control it anymore. I'm sick and tired of not being enough. For my parents. For the people I thought were my friends. And most of all, for myself. I don't want to live like that anymore, being in someone else's shadow, namely my sisters."

"And you don't have to. You're a strong, smart, and very capable woman. You can do anything. If your mom can't see that, then it's her loss." I pause, as she looks uncertain, and I get that. She's so young. She's not street smart at all, she's barely lived. She has no idea how cruel the real world can be, yet she seems to have suffered a lot of it just from the people closest to her. My chest constricts and a protective urge flares through me.

Fuck.

Am I fucking doomed?

"Maybe she'll have calmed down and will see your side," I go on. "She might learn from this and be a little nicer to you."

She laughs. "You don't know my mom. My dad isn't as bad, but he's not exactly Father of the Year."

I don't want to persuade her into doing anything. She has to make the decision for herself. "Have you thought about moving out? Maybe you'd have a better relationship with your parents if you weren't under their roof. Do they pay for school?"

She shakes her head. "They were hoping I'd get a scholarship for college, but I dropped my application and decided to go to get my real estate certification, much to my parents' disgust, and I'm paying my own tuition."

I stare at her, wondering how this young woman has the weight of the world on her shoulders. She probably can't afford to live on her own.

This is the time she should be enjoying her youth. Studying and making new friends, experiencing life and partying. Not acting like she's a fifty-year-old woman.

She needs to let loose.

"If I got a second job," she goes on. "Maybe I could rent a room somewhere…I could ask around. I've made a couple of friends in town. They might know of somewhere."

I nod. "I just don't want you going back home if they're going to hammer you when you get there."

There's that smile again.

"What?" I say, bumping her hips.

"You're worried about me?"

I smile too, I can't help it. "You seem to have that effect on me, if you haven't noticed already."

"I kinda have." She laughs. "And I think I like it."

We kiss for a long time, my hands roaming down to cup her ass. Her lips are like soft pillows, so succulent and ripe for the picking. I want to be her first. I have to be.

But I don't want to hurt her. I don't want to promise her

things I can't give her, even though I don't want anyone else to have it either.

I'm so confused.

I grind her into my hard-on and her lips part, a small moan leaving her throat.

"I loved it when you called my name the other night," I mumble against her lips. "When I made you come for the first time."

She moans again, whispering, "Hutch." My dick hardens further, proving my point.

"I want more of you," I tell her.

"I want that too," she whispers.

"Do you know what I'm askin' you, baby girl?"

"Yes."

"And you want me to give it to you?"

The thought…fuck me…

"I want it to be you," she whispers.

I take a long breath. "Even if I can't give you more?"

Her eyes meet mine. "I know you're a bad boy, from the wrong side of the tracks, Hutch. You're in a motorcycle club. I'm not dumb. I'm not stupid enough to believe we have a future together. But right now, I just want to be with you. Like that."

I smile against her lips. I want to tell her she's not stupid.

I wish I could also tell her that I think the future might

be looking a bit brighter now, but I'm afraid I'm just acting on impulse.

"You sure sound a lot more confident than the first time I saw you," I muse. "I wasn't sure if you wanted to jump me or slap me silly."

"I've never met a guy like you before…"

"A guy like me?"

She looks down. "A guy who's… sexy."

My lips turn up. It's nothing I haven't heard before, but coming out of her mouth, it feels different.

"You think I'm sexy?"

Her eyes meet mine as she narrows them. "I think you already know it."

I grin. "I didn't know that's how you feel."

"Well, now you do."

I love how much more confident she is. It warms my heart. "And you believe me when I say you're beautiful and I love your body, without shyin' away from me?"

Her throat bobs as she swallows. "I'll try not to shy away."

"What about believin' me?"

"I'll try that too."

"I want to bury myself inside you, Kirsty. How do you feel about that?"

I hear her intake of breath. "I…uh…"

I cup her face once more as she squeezes her arms

around me. "Just say yes."

"Y-yes," she breathes. "But I've got no experience…I don't know how to…"

"I'll teach you. I'll show you what to do and what I like," I say, holding back a groan at the very idea of popping her cherry. "And in turn, you'll tell me what you want me to do and what you like."

"I…I don't know what I like."

I kiss her lightly, enjoying her innocence. I'm basking in it.

"You will, baby. Oh, you will."

"You seem pretty sure."

I bite down on my lip. "Did you like what I did to you the other night?"

She swallows again, then slowly nods.

I groan at the memory of how slick she was, how she tasted when I sucked my fingers later, and how my cock felt when I spurted all over myself, imagining it was her squeezing my dick and not my own hand.

"Well, it'll be like that, except better."

"Better?"

I move my mouth to her ear. "I'll use my mouth where my hand was." She intakes a sharp breath once again. "And my tongue where my fingers went."

"Oh, God."

"It's a whole new sensation. And you'd better get used to me using your body for pleasure, baby girl, because I want to own every single one of those moments when you lose it."

I nip her neck with my teeth.

"Hutch," she whispers. I can practically smell her arousal. I'm so turned on. But our first time isn't gonna be here, up against a tree, on the ground or against my bike. I want to be in a bed where I can move around, take her body how I want to, and take my time.

"Yeah, you'll be sayin' that name a lot from now on." I wonder if she'll want to taste me too. I get that it'll be scary for her; my cock isn't exactly a small thing, but I want her to suck me off. I want all of her firsts.

We hold each other, and when it starts to get dark, I take my cut off and wrap it around her shoulders.

No woman has ever worn my cut before.

I can't say my heart doesn't do a flip in my chest when I see her wearing it. My name on the patch. It looks good on her.

Fuck me.

"I should take you home."

She nods. "I shouldn't make my parents worry."

I pull her close again. "When can I see you again?"

She smiles softly. "Soon."]

"When?" I grip her ass. I need you.

"I'll get away somehow. We can meet at the cafe. The day after tomorrow."

"Why not sooner?" I know I sound like a whiny little bitch.

"I've got class."

Good. "You better be there," I say as our mouths meet once more. "Or I will come find you."

"Is that a threat?"

I brush her hair back and tuck it behind her ears. "No, darlin', that's a promise."

BRACKEN RIDGE
REBELS
ARIZONA
M · C

CHAPTER 9

KIRSTY

ONE WEEK LATER

Facing my parents was hard.

I never wanted it to be this way, but the way they've been treating me for such a long time is not right. I'm not a child. And it's taken my whole life for me to be able to stand up to them.

I've never given my parents any grief. I've always done exactly what they said, behaved like a good middle-class girl should. I've never been wild and free. But all that changed the minute Richie Hutchison stepped into my life.

Now he's all I can think about.

That night, I did go home. And I told my parents I would be moving out.

To say they were shocked was an understatement. My mom wouldn't even talk to me and that suited me fine.

One of the girls I worked with told me she was moving out of her apartment, it's above a pub called the Stone Crow. According to Felicia, her rent was cheap since she agreed to clean the pub after hours, and Steph, the owner, was kind and fair. I jumped at the offer.

I stare at the box of things on my floor, and I wonder what the hell has gotten into me.

I can't help but smile. I've been the happiest I've ever been, and I'm also shitting my pants.

Hutch and I have stolen moments in the cafe here and there, but I haven't been able to really see him while I've been packing my stuff. Adding the fact that I've fallen for the bad boy biker, the one who took part in threatening my own father, wouldn't exactly go down well. And really, there's no point adding salt to the wounds.

I want to be with Hutch, but I know he doesn't feel the way I do. I know this can't last. I'm not stupid enough to have my head so far in the clouds that I don't understand we're from two different worlds. But that doesn't mean I can't enjoy myself in the process. I just have to guard my heart. Not let him see exactly what he's doing to me and how much I hang onto his every word.

It's a lot of power to give someone, and when he breaks my heart, I really hope I'll be able to recover quickly. I know I'll come out the other end, so by preparing for the fallout now, I can protect my heart a little bit more.

I haven't told him that it's my birthday this coming Saturday, and when Callie and Helen invite me to a party, I'm feeling all kinds of bad girl vibes when they convince me to say yes.

For the first time ever, I wear makeup. My mom was always against it, never allowing me to experiment with cosmetics, so I've never tried.

Callie helps create a smoky look on my eyes and she paints my lips cherry red. I dress in the tight jeans I've never had the guts to wear, except for in the privacy of my bedroom, and I wear a long-sleeve, fitted top with sheer sleeves. I stand back to admire myself. I can hardly believe I'm the same woman from a few weeks ago.

I feel good.

For the first time in years, I feel good about my body.

When Helen and Callie heard all about Hutch - yes, I couldn't keep him a secret from them any longer - they also made me see I'm not the big, horrible frump I thought I was. I even have a waist, and it looks pretty good in these jeans.

I'll always have hips. I'll always have boobs. I'll always have an ass, and I'm okay with that…I also like that Hutch likes it. If I'm honest, tonight I'm dressing for him. He just doesn't know I'm showing up at the clubhouse…that's where the party is heading.

To say I'm terrified is an understatement, but Helen and Callie told me they've been to a couple of parties before, and the bikers were there. Helen is sweet on a guy named Hank, so she's hoping to hook up with him tonight.

I don't know what Hutch will think. Hopefully, he won't be mad that I've turned up at his clubhouse without being invited, but I can't go another minute until I can be with him. And tonight could be the night.

Doing a twirl in the mirror, I laugh at my own giddiness.

"You're just happy because you want Hutch to pop your cherry," Callie says.

I slap her on the arm lightly. "I do not!"

"Do too. Ugh, there are so many hot guys in that club. Don't get me wrong, there's old cruddies there too, so stay away from them," she warns. "But Hutch, he's packing. How far are you gonna let him go?"

"I'm not," I lie. "I just want to get a look at him. He'll probably have other women dripping all over him to even notice me." The words feel like poison, but I can't let my friends know just how deeply I feel for him. And if I do actually see him with other women hanging off him, I don't know what I'd do.

I don't want to even ask him if he's slept with anyone else since we made out. I don't want the answer. I don't want to ruin the fantasy I have in my head.

Because in my head, it's perfect. And that's how I want it to stay.

We head out, stopping by at one of Helen's friend's houses who's having a party. I've never had a proper drink before, so when someone hands me a glass of clear liquid, I smell it hesitantly.

"Are you going to drink that?" Helen laughs.

I screw up my nose and shake my head. "What is it?"

She sniffs it too, then says, "Tequila."

I pass the shot glass to her.

I don't want to be drunk or anywhere near it when I see Hutch. I want to remember everything about tonight.

So we weave through the crowd, dance, laugh, and mingle. And not one person looks at me sideways over what I'm wearing or how big my ass might look in these jeans. Nobody cares.

I start to think if most of this has been in my head all along, then I remember my sister and my mom, and I quickly shake the memories away.

My mom didn't even come to my work to say happy birthday. I stopped by my dad's shop, and he gave me an awkward one-armed hug but that was it. To say disappointment radiated off him was an understatement. But I don't care.

My parents can think what they want.

Hours later, when we're laughing so hard that my sides hurt, Helen announces we're leaving.

We walk a mile down the road, since none of us can drive, toward the deserted street that leads to the clubhouse.

When we get there, I start to think it wasn't such a good idea that we came. The place bustling with people. There are motorcycles everywhere, as well as cars in the lot, and music so loud you could probably hear it in Mesa.

"Are we sure we really wanna do this?" I question, as we all stand at the gates like lost puppies. "I mean, once we go in there, can we get out?"

My friends laugh. "The boys won't mind," Callie says. "The more girls the merrier. We just have to stick together, agreed?"

Helen and I both nod. "Agreed," we say in unison.

"And for Christ's sake, Helen," Callie goes on. "Try not to let Hank get to second base before Kirsty and I leave your side."

Helen elbows her in the ribs as I laugh.

These girls are my tribe. I can't believe it's taken me this long to find a couple of girls I actually like and who get me. It's a game changer when you have girlfriends to talk to, laugh with, who don't judge you.

When the biker on the gate wearing a leather jacket labeled 'Prospect' gives us the once over, he lets us in without any words exchanged. It seems a little too easy.

The music gets louder as we approach, and when we make it through the doors, the entire place is in complete disarray. There are bodies literally everywhere.

A band played on a makeshift stage off to the side with people dancing around and head banging in front.

he bar inside is full of bikers, women, and other people

just dressed normally. I know straight away we may have walked into trouble.

Clutching onto my friends, we scurry across the room. I keep my head down, afraid to meet anyone's eye in case they approach us. I'm really thinking this was a very bad idea.

The music pounds in my ears and people dance all around us, screaming, wailing, and laughing. At least they seem to know how to have a good time.

We settle across the room, in the shadows, but when I look around to try to spot Hutch, I see a wake of bikers looking our way.

Uh oh.

"Are you sure this was a good idea?" I ask the girls, just as one of the guys, a tall, skinny dude with the word 'Spyder' written across his motorcycle jacket approaches.

"Hey, girls," he says, giving us a grin that reminds me of the Cheshire Cat. "You new around here?"

Oh great. The worst pick up line ever.

"Hank knows we're coming," Helen pipes up, even though Hank doesn't know, but at least it seems like we were sort of invited.

His eyes skate over Callie and then me as he rubs his chin. "Sure, he's right over by the bar."

We both give Helen a pointed look and she stays where she is. "I'll look for him shortly."

If they leave me standing here alone, I will literally make a run for it.

Spyder, however, doesn't leave.

Looking back up at him, he gives me a chin lift. Oh no.

I smile awkwardly. "What's your name?" he asks, shouting over the music.

"Uh…" I glance at my friends who look about as scared as I do. "Um, Kirsty."

He looks me up and down in a way that makes me cringe. It's nothing like how Hutch looks at me.

"Great. You wanna suck some cock?" He cups his crotch as my eyes go wide.

Shit.

Shit. Shit. Shit!

Before I get to respond, someone taps him on the shoulder and when he turns, I watch as Hutch headbutts him in the face, sending him flying backwards, landing on the people behind him.

All of us girls shriek and jump back in shock.

The guy named Spyder starts bleeding from his nose.

"Fuck, man! What the fuck was that for?"

He points at me, his face furious. "She's mine."

"Don't see no cut on her back."

"Doesn't need one. I'm tellin' you right here, right now, keep your hands off. Got me?"

"What the fuck, Hutch?" He holds his nose as a scantily

clad woman comes running up, a towel in her hands. "I was just messin' with her."

It's clear by the sheer size of Hutch compared to his counterpart, that he's going to win if this breaks out into a fight. Hutch is a big, solid guy. Even though he's young, he's burly for his age.

"You wanna piece of me?" His face is red, angry, and he's wearing some of Spyder's blood across his face.

Spyder shakes his head. "Nah, man, I'm sorry. Calm the fuck down!"

Hutch doesn't help him up, instead he comes toward me, his eyes skating down my body at my outfit. "Kirsty, what the hell are you doing here?"

I open my mouth, then close it again.

He's mad.

I messed up.

I shouldn't have come here.

It was a mistake…but then…he just said I was his, right?

"I'm with Hank," Helen says quickly as his eyes dart to her. "We came to celebrate Kirsty's birthday."

He switches his gaze back to me. "It's your birthday?"

I nod, unable to speak.

He comes closer, but I move backwards.

He frowns. "Why didn't you tell me?"

"I…I don't know," I say shakily.

I need to go.

He just headbutted another man, who picks himself up and gets led away by the woman with barely any clothes on. Hutch doesn't bat an eyelid.

"Well, baby girl," he says, his mouth moving closer to my ear. "You've got about thirty seconds to explain it to me."

He uses my words back at me that I said to him the night he climbed through my bedroom window.

Oh, the irony.

And I've no idea what the hell to say to that.

Hutch

BRACKEN RIDGE
REBELS
ARIZONA
M · C

CHAPTER 10

HUTCH

I stare down at Kirsty, shaking with rage.

I wish I knew what came over me, but where other men and her are concerned, I can't rein in my temper.

That'll be the last time Spyder ever talks to her. His disgusting, lewd comments make bile rise in my throat. The only man allowed to talk dirty to her is me. The only man who will ever be able to talk dirty to her is me. I'll fuck him up if he looks at her ever again.

I wait for her answer, ignoring Grim as he tries to pass me a wad of napkins so I can wipe the blood off my face.

"I…uh…we…it just sort of happened…"

I give her a firm look, then, taking pity on her, I say, "Need to get you out of here."

She frowns. "It's not safe?"

I take a look around me. "No. You and your friends need to follow me."

Her eyes go wide as I grab her arm with one hand, wiping my face with the other.

"But…Helen needs to see Hank…"

"She can do that another time," I reply, heading straight for the back entrance, as there'll be less people there to navigate through.

Lord help me if Spyder shows back up again. I've heard enough of his shit over the last year or two and I'm ready to gut him if I hear one more word.

I practically drag Kirsty from the room, her friends tagging along behind. At least they're listening, I suppose. Something about their faces tells me that they got more than they bargained for by coming here tonight. They may think they're being wild and cool turning up here, but all they are is pussy on a plate for some of the brothers in this club. And I don't want that on my conscience.

I don't like Hank, never have. He's a first-class asshole, but what her friend decides to do is up to her. I don't want Kirsty here, and that's saying a lot. This is my club. These are my brothers, the place I call home.

Worst of all, it hits me with full force that she doesn't belong here. That she sticks out like a sore thumb. Maybe I don't want to face it because I like being around her so much, but maybe I'm to blame for this.

I didn't intentionally lead her on. Sure, I admit, I wanted to fuck her, and I told her as such, but now that I've seen what a sweet, kind person she is, I'm not so sure this is just about fucking any more.

I don't do this.

I don't do the girlfriend thing.

But I can honestly say I've had fuckin' heart palpitations when being with this one. I've sat around thinking about whether she got home safe. What she's doing. Or when I'm gonna see her again. If I even have a shot.

It isn't right.

She shouldn't be embroiled in this party, with the club and most of all, with me.

Fuck.

When we make it outside, I shrug off Dog and Scrooge. They take one look at my face and keep walking. Sometimes it feels like I'm the Enforcer around here, instead of Harlem, but I roll with it. They know better than to start shit with me when I'm angry. I'm like a bull.

I won't stop until the other man is down and doesn't get back up again.

When we're safe enough away, I turn to the girls. "No cabs around here, I'll walk you home."

"But we just got…"

"Callie," Kirsty confirms. "Hutch is right, it was pretty wild in there."

She gives her friend a pointed look. "Coming from the guy who just headbutted his club brother?"

I toss the napkins in the trash can next to me. "Trust me, sweetheart, I did y'all a favor. I'm gonna grab my sled. Wait here.”

I take off to the back lot, kick the stand up, crab walking my motorcycle so I can get out front, back to the girls.

They’re still waiting near the gate where I left them.

Kirsty still looks a little shell-shocked.

“You’re really going to walk us home?” Helen says, looking from me to Kirsty.

“Hurry up and get movin’, before I change my mind,” I say. “How far away do you live?”

“About a ten-minute walk,” Callie replies.

I grunt.

Great.

We start walking and I push my sled out of the gate, much to the prospect’s surprise, and we follow the deserted road back in the direction of town.

Her two friends walk ahead of us.

“How’s your face?” she asks after a few long moments of silence.

“It’s fine.”

“You hit that guy pretty hard.”

“Not as hard as I’d like to.”

I’m still mad. She shouldn’t have come. And Spyder was asking for it.

“Are you gonna stay mad at me all night?” Kirsty asks, peeking sideways as our eyes meet.

“Maybe.”

She frowns. "I didn't think…"

"No, you didn't think, Kirst, and I'm mad at you. You could've told me that's what you were plannin', and I could've warned you not to come."

"But why? What would have happened?"

"Trust me, not all my brothers in there are willing to keep their hands off, especially when young, fresh meat show up, ripe for the picking."

She wrinkles her nose, causing me to chuckle.

It's really not funny.

I'm only glad Scar didn't see. I would've had some explaining to do.

Technically, if a woman isn't your ol' lady or hasn't been claimed by you, she's fair game.

All the women who show up to the club know what they're there for. Sex.

The fact these girls arrived because they're young, naive and don't understand club life is yet just another indication of why I should end whatever this is.

I know I'm to blame. She's only nineteen; she's inexperienced, and I was about to lead her down a very dark path, knowing she'd come, willingly.

"That doesn't sound great."

"It isn't."

A long silence follows. "Do you like my outfit?"

I glance down at her body. Her ass is fuckin' delicious

in those tight jeans. I want to grab hold of it, spank it until it's pink, and then fuck her from behind. But I can't now.

I've somehow grown a conscience and I'm re-thinking what I'm even doing right this very minute.

"Why do you think I'm takin' you home?"

Her eyes light up, not exactly catching my meaning.

I know she wants me. I know that look. And I want her too.

I wrestle with the idea that I should have let her down gently. I should never have crept into her room and done those things. That only makes this harder.

Now I've had Kirsty heroin and I'm not sure if I can stop, even if my intentions aren't as pure as I'm trying to make out.

I snort. There ain't nothing pure about me. Her, however…

She glances at me. "Is something funny?"

"Nope."

"Are you laughing at me?"

I shake my head. "No, I'm laughing at the irony of all of this. I'm a walking cliche, baby girl, and here I am, bein' the good guy, makin' sure you get home safe."

She looks straight ahead. "You want to know what I think?"

This should be good. "Shoot."

"I think you're not all that."

My eyebrows quirk.

"I think you're all talk," she goes on, as if I needed more clarification. "You're actually a good guy deep down, but you run with this dirty, low-down club, and people just think you're a bad person because that's the persona you portray."

Wow. Nobody's ever come straight out and said that to my face.

The fact that I've struggled with the morals of this club and what we do has never been apparent to anybody…until now.

"You finished?"

"No," she snaps, keeping her voice low. "I really don't think that a man like you would sneak up into my room and not even try to…try to…"

"Fuck you?"

"Yes! Exactly. You're a good guy, and you don't let anyone see it because you have to be this other person to be accepted. Trust me when I say I know. I've done it my whole entire life, and it's not fun."

"You think I'm in this club because I want to be accepted?"

"Don't you? What's the point of a club if you don't want to belong somewhere?"

Fuck, she's smart too.

"I hurt your dad," I remind her. She won't be so

complimentary now…

"But you didn't. You partook in going there, yes, but you didn't hurt him."

"Same difference. I was there."

Shit, if she's noticed I'm half pussy-whipped, maybe my club brothers have too.

She shakes her head. "You don't have to lie to me, Richie, I can see right through you. This isn't you."

"It is me!" I whisper-shout. "And I don't appreciate you messin' with my head. I was fine before you came along. I could fuck pussy every night of the week. Now you're in my head, I haven't even…"

She stares at me, her mouth gaping. Instead of being shocked by my words, she asks, "You haven't had sex with anyone…like lately?"

I glance at her friends, realizing they're chatting away ahead of us, I turn my attention back to her. "No, I haven't, and that right there tells you just how fucked in the head I am that I'm even admitting that to you." I shake my head, trying to make sense of it myself.

A small smile plays on her lips as she tries to hide it. I shake my head. "Oh, you think that's funny, Kirsty?" She bites down on her lip. "You think that tuggin' on my dick with my hand instead of what I usually do is humorous? You think goin' home that night after I fingered you in your bedroom with a full cream in my pants is funny, baby girl?"

I see desire in her eyes as she glances at me, looking up at me under those long lashes.

Her face…she's just so…no! She's not anything…stop this madness…

She leans into me, bumping my shoulder. "It is a little bit funny."

I shake my head, my cock hardening because I'm mad at her.

I know I still want her. She's asking for it.

"I'm gonna remember you said that," I mutter as we take the rest of the way in complete silence.

It seems to take ages, but we finally get to her friends' place. After saying their goodnights, I go to start my sled so I can take her home too, but instead, I kick the stand down and turn to Kirsty as she steps back suddenly, sensing my current mood.

My eyes are blazing as I walk her back toward the tree, pressing her up against it, caging her in.

"Now seems like a good time to discuss me bein' all talk," I growl, my hands on either side of her head as I clutch the branches above me.

"Now probably isn't a good time," she starts.

I put my finger up to her lips to silence her. "And that whole thing about you laughin' at me."

"I wasn't laughing!" she muffles, yelping as I pinch her chin.

"It's my turn to talk now, baby girl. I think you've said enough tonight."

She eyeballs me, and quite frankly, I dig it. Chicks never give it to me straight, and I find this oddly impressive that she's doing it.

"Somethin' about me bein' a good guy? And I don't let anyone see it…"

She stands her ground, defying me by not looking away.

My dick hardens.

"You got anythin' else to say out of that smart mouth of yours?"

She shakes her head. "You said it was your turn to talk…so…no."

"Wise-ass." I lean in and catch her bottom lip with my teeth and tug on it. "I told you what bitin' down on your lip does to me." I grab her hand and place her palm on the bulge at the front of my jeans. "Does that feel like I'm not all that?" She says nothing, her eyes doing all the talking.

"Does it feel like I'm all talk?" Again, nothing. I press my forehead against hers. "I want to fuck you so bad."

"Then do it," she whispers.

I shake my head. "You don't know what you're sayin'."

"Yes, I do, Hutch. I can't stop thinking about you too… about what we did…what you said…how I feel when I'm with you…"

"You shouldn't say those things."

"But it's the truth."

"You're young. You haven't really lived yet…"

"I don't need you to tell me that. This is what I'm trying to do, live. Taking risks, making mistakes, it's all part of growing up. I want to experience all of it."

And she wants to do it with me.

"Not like this. This kind of mistake tonight could've turned out very, very differently if I hadn't seen you come in."

"But you did."

"Those guys…they're not all good…"

"I meant with you. I want all of those firsts with you, Hutch, nobody else could ever compare."

I stare at her, comprehending her words, knowing I should walk away. It's now or never.

I should do the right thing. I should let her down gently… Instead, I say, "Baby girl, you did a bad, bad thing."

BRACKEN RIDGE
REBELS
ARIZONA
M · C

CHAPTER 11

KIRSTY

"What about you?" I counter. "You did a bad thing too." His lips twitch. I know I'm talking back, and he seems to enjoy it when I do.

"I did a lot of bad things," he grunts, his eyes flicking down to my mouth. "None of which you'd probably care to know about."

I bite down on my lip again, releasing it suddenly when I remember what he said.

His mouth turns into a slight pout. "You did it again."

"I didn't mean to."

"Do I make you nervous?" He presses his bulge into my stomach, and my breath hitches.

"No," I lie.

He smirks. "I think I do."

"I think I make you nervous."

He chuckles. "You got a mouth on you, Kirst, and I think I like it." I gasp as his thumb swipes over my lips, smearing my lipstick. "I don't like this, though."

"I wore it for you."

He grunts. "The only way red is gonna look good on you, baby girl, is if it's wrapped around my dick."

My eyes go wide.

I don't even have time to respond when his lips crash onto mine, as I open my mouth and let him in. He grunts, the sexy noise doing things to my insides as he pushes me farther into the tree. I feel every inch of him, my hand still cupping the bulge that's driving me insane. I give him a squeeze, and he growls louder.

"I'm supposed to be takin' you home," he mutters when we pull apart. "Not drivin' you into the goddamn tree."

"Take me home," I breathe, my words having a double meaning.

"Kirst…"

"I want it to be you, Hutch, please." I know I sound like I'm begging, but I don't care.

I've never wanted anything quite so much as I do this man in front of me.

All coherent thoughts go out the window where he's concerned. I know I want this.

I start to move my palm against his wood, and he moves off a little, his eyes flicking down at my movements.

"See what you do to me, Kirst?"

I nod, loving that I'm making him crazy.

"I wanted to spank your ass tonight," he mumbles, his

hands moving to cup my face. "What do you think about that?"

I squeeze him harder, and he hisses in response. "I think I want your hands on me."

He groans, still watching as my hand works him over. My nipples pebble and one hand moves down to grope my breast. "Fuck, baby."

He takes my mouth again, his tongue touching mine, and we get lost in the moment until he pulls back suddenly, removing my hand from him.

"Need to get to a bed…now."

My heart accelerates as he pushes off the tree, taking my hand as he moves over to the motorcycle. Handing me the helmet, he hops on and kicks up the stand, starting the engine.

I climb on behind him, pressing up against this large, warm body, and I don't hear what he mutters under his breath, but whatever it is has me smiling.

He can deny it all he wants, but we have something. This isn't just about sex. If it were, then why didn't he nail me in my bedroom that night instead of disappearing out the window. It would have been the ultimate revenge toward my dad. But I know he's not like that, I don't know how, I just feel it.

I meant what I said. I do think he's a good guy, I just don't really like the company he keeps.

Knowing that, I still went there, and it doesn't change

how I feel about him.

We take off from the curb like a bat out of hell, and he drives me to the back of the Stone Crow, where he parks and turns the engine off.

I immediately dismount, yanking off my helmet as he stares straight ahead. When he doesn't say anything, I squeeze his arm. "Hutch?"

His eyes find mine. "I planned on walkin' away," he says, shocking me. "I didn't want to, I thought it was for the best…but now…"

"Now?"

He runs a hand through his hair. "Now I want what I want."

I swallow hard. "And that is?" My breathing accelerates when he swings one leg over the bike.

"You."

My heart beats so fast that I'm sure it could explode out of my chest at any moment.

Without words, he takes my hand and proceeds very quickly to the backdoor. I have my key in my hand by the time we reach it, my hands shaking as I try three times to get the key in the damn lock.

Chuckling, Hutch takes the key from me and says, "You sure I don't make you nervous?" He gives me a wink that makes my stomach flutter.

I don't have the guts to reply. All of a sudden, things are

getting very real.

Once we're inside, he points upstairs, and I nod.

He's never been in my apartment, obviously. No boy ever has.

When we get to the top of the landing, I start to fiddle with the buttons on my shirt.

He uses the other key on the ring to get inside.

When he scans the room for a moment, his eyes come back to mine as he closes the door, holding his hand on it like it's final.

And maybe it is.

I'm nervous. I'm scared. But I want this.

I reach for him. "I'm ready, Hutch."

He presses his forehead to mine. "You sure you haven't cast some kinda spell on me, baby girl?"

I smile as he walks me back into the door, pressing one hand at my throat.

"You can't go wearing outfits like this again," he tells me. "Ever."

I nod. "All right."

He smirks. "All of a sudden the cat's got your tongue?"

I shake my head, my chest rising and falling rapidly.

"Shouldn't have come," he tells me, his voice low. "Kirsty."

"I'm here," I breathe.

He nuzzles his nose into my neck, releasing me, caging

me in once more. My hands flatten against the door as I struggle to control my breathing.

"Nothing has to happen that you don't choose."

My pulse quickens.

I want it all…I wish I could voice that, but the words won't form.

"And you have to tell me if I do something you don't like, understand?"

I nod.

"Let me hear you, Kirsty."

"Yes," I whisper.

He kisses my neck with an open mouth, sucking on the skin. I know it'll leave a mark and I think he does too. He just doesn't care.

His hands leave the door and cup my face as his lips move to mine, kissing me gently at first, testing, tasting. When our tongues meet, I hear the rumble he makes, turning my insides to mush.

This is why.

This is exactly why.

Because of how he makes me feel.

Because of what he's doing to me right now.

Because he's the only man I'll ever want.

I bravely move my hands from the door and plant them on his chest, feeling his muscles beneath my fingers. Reveling in his touch, I moan when he nips my bottom lip.

His hands move down lower, cupping my breasts, squeezing them as he pushes his hard-on into me.

Sliding my hands up to his shoulders, I shove his jacket off, and he lifts away for a moment so he can shrug his arms out.

I lift the hem of his shirt as he raises his arms once more. Then I pull it over his head, throwing it purposely behind him.

My eyes flick down his gorgeous body. He has a splay of tattoos across his chest. An eagle. A cross. A skull.

Several patterns with roses and thorns. I trace them with my fingers as he watches me, a small smile on his face.

"Do you know how beautiful you look touchin' me, baby girl?"

I flick my eyes back to his. "Your body is…" I can't even finish.

He smirks. "I work out."

"I can see that."

I flatten my palms across his pecs, squeezing as he watches me intently.

"Do you like what you see, Kirst?"

Nodding, I run my hands down to his abs. Holy crap, this man is built like a machine. I've never seen a body like his before; not even the fittest boys in school on the football team look this good.

I lose all sense of reality as I run my hand farther south,

through the smattering of hair at his navel. All the while, his eyes bore into mine.

I see how he sees me.

I believe him when he tells me I'm beautiful because his eyes don't lie.

He doesn't lie.

If that makes me naive and stupid, fine, I'll take it, but I know what I see and what I feel.

Testing his resolve, I run my palm down past his belt buckle and over his zipper. The bulge is huge, literally huge. I've no idea what the hell to do with that thing, but the hiss that leaves his lips makes me feel like I'm his queen and it doesn't matter. Like he said; he'll teach me.

"That's it, baby," he mutters, and now it's his turn to bite down on his lip. "Can you feel what you do to me?" I nod. "Can you feel what this hot, beautiful, sexy body does to me?" I nod again. "Unzip me."

My eyes flick to him, and a flash of worry must cross my features, because he adds, "It's okay, it won't bite."

I smile softly, feeling the heat rise in my cheeks. He helps by unbuckling his belt and letting it fall open, then he undoes the top button of his jeans.

Biting down on my lip, I move my fingers to his zipper. Straight away, I see a dark flock of hair, and then skin…he's not wearing any underwear.

"Holy crap," I whisper.

He chuckles, then helps me out by shrugging his jeans down all the way, letting them fall to his feet.

My eyes almost bug out of their sockets as I stare at his penis. His forehead presses against mine as he touches himself, moving his hand up and down his shaft a couple of times.

My face is beet red. I can feel it and the blood pounding in my ears.

It's so big.

"Ummm," I start.

He chuckles. "You gonna touch it?"

My eyes flick up to his as he grins at me. I think he likes shocking me.

He leans down and takes his boots off, pulling his socks free and tugs his jeans fully off. Standing before me butt naked, while I'm still fully clothed, I don't know where to look. He's not shy about his body.

He reaches to my lip to free it from my teeth, then with the other hand, he grabs mine and places it on his dick. I gasp.

It's smooth in my hand, thick, and so damn hard. I can't stop staring at it.

He hisses when I squeeze, then says, "Like this, baby girl." Placing his hand over mine, he starts to move it up and down, essentially jerking him off, his tongue wasting no time finding mine as he kisses me roughly. Hungrily.

And I can't get enough of it.

My other hand clutches his bicep as he groans. His other hand reaches to my blouse, and he tries to undo it with one hand as I jerk him harder. Getting frustrated, I hear a tear, and I look down to see he's ripped my blouse in half and the buttons fly off everywhere.

"Sorry," he mutters, looking anything but.

I don't care. I want him to touch me too.

I pull my torn blouse from my body, revealing my black bra. Moving his mouth down my neck, he kisses the top of my breasts, his fingers moving south to my jeans. He undoes the top button as I kick my shoes off, my hand in his hair, tugging on it as I moan into his mouth.

I'm so wet, I can feel it, and I hope he likes it. He seemed to, the last time we did this.

Except now I'm going to have his giant penis inside me. The thing grows even bigger in my hand as I keep jerking him off. Now I've got the hang of it, he lets go.

"Slower, Kirst," he mutters, as my zipper's being lowered. "Or I'll come all over you before I even get it inside your sweet pussy."

I close my eyes at his dirty words and do as he says. Everything about him oozes sex. And for tonight, I want to be his, any way I can get him.

He tugs my jeans down, my underwear too, and I still... never being this bare in front of anyone before.

His eyes stay on my face. "You okay?"

I nod.

"Words, Kirsty."

"Yes," I whisper.

He smiles, reaches around to my back, and unclips my bra.

Instinctively, my arms fold over my chest, trying to hide myself from him, but he's not having it. He holds my wrists and moves them aside so he can stare down at me.

"Fuck," he mutters.

My breasts hang heavily as he stares at them, then he flicks his eyes lower, and my face flames red as I hide in the crook of his shoulder.

He skims his hands down my body, cupping my breasts briefly, then he moves one hand farther, over my stomach, toward the apex of my thighs. I reach down and stop him, holding his wrist as his eyes shoot back to mine.

"Baby girl?"

I'm panting so hard, I may pass out.

"I'm okay," I whisper. "Just nervous."

His smile crinkles. "Can I touch you?"

I bite down on my lip as he frowns. Releasing it quickly, I say, "Yes."

Still holding his wrist with one hand, he moves it lower, skating his fingers over my sensitive flesh as I make a noise I know I've never made before.

This is it, I tell myself. And I hope to God I don't blow it.

I want it too much.

I want him so much.

I will remember this night forever.

BRACKEN RIDGE
REBELS
ARIZONA
M · C

CHAPTER 12

HUTCH

I can barely breathe.

She's so beautiful. Her body is soft and round. Her tits are perfect.

Her ass…I can't even go there. Yet, she doesn't know it.

I don't know why she still tries to cover herself up. I have to keep knocking her hands out the way.

Her hand begins to move on my cock again, and it's taking all of my control not to throw her on the bed and ravage her stupid.

When my fingers move through her pussy lips, and I feel how wet she is, I groan loudly.

She crosses her other arm over her body, trying to hide her stomach from my view.

I lean into her ear. "Don't ever hide from me," I tell her. "This body is mine, Kirsty Mason. Tell me."

She takes a moment, her breath catching in her throat. "It's yours," she whispers.

"And who am I, when I touch you like this?"

"Richie."

I nip her ear with my teeth as she yelps, then I scoop her up into my arms as she wraps her arms around me.

"Wrap your legs around me, baby. That's it."

She does as she's told, and I start to kiss her, moving toward the bed. Laying her down as she lets go, she scrambles backwards as I stare at her. I crawl onto the mattress as I move closer, every move I make predatory.

My cock hangs heavily and angrily between my legs, and as her eyes dip down, they widen slightly. I know she must be terrified, but I'm not just gonna fuck her like an amateur. She'll never get that from me. I know how to please a woman. And I plan on enjoying every second of this.

I move over the top of her as she wets her lips, her throat bobbing, then she says, "Can we turn the light off?"

There's a small lamp to the side of the bed, barely letting any light in.

I shake my head. "No."

"But…"

"No buts. I want to see you, all of you."

I spread her legs, coming up onto my knees as she tries to close them.

"Don't hide," I warn. "I want you to see how much I desire you, baby girl, what a bad girl you've been, turnin' me on like this with that curvy, sexy body of yours. If you hide from me again, I'll spank your ass."

I hear her breath hitch as I move down over the top of her, kissing her quickly, then I press kisses onto her jaw, her neck, all the way down to her breasts. I cup them, squeezing them together and thumbing her nipples. They're hard, pink, and need my attention.

She groans when I flick them, rubbing them back and forth as she bucks off the bed.

"You like that, baby?"

She nods.

I move my mouth over one taut nipple, sucking hard, then I do the exact same thing to the other one. She just about combusts then and there.

I go back and forth between the two, sucking, nipping, licking as she watches me.

"I bet I could make you come just like this," I mutter, latching on while I move one hand between her legs.

She's dripping. Her slickness coating her thighs as I groan, imaging my cock sinking deep inside her. Her first time. I'm gonna be her first and the last.

I play with her clit, stroking, as I stare down at her mound, her pink skin glistening. I know she's close.

"Come for me," I mutter, knowing she needs release. "Let me hear you."

Her hands clutch my ass, clenching as she starts to climax. She squeezes her eyes shut, and it's like euphoria just watching her. I ride her through it, sweat forming on her brow as I feel quite smug with myself. She cries out, her climax taking her over as I watch with satisfaction.

My cock can't take much more…

"Good girl."

She pants, trying to get her breath back as I leave her glorious tits and kiss her stomach, taking my time as she pants and writhes underneath me. I press both my hands on either side of her knees, pressing her spread eagled and move my mouth to her pussy.

Fuck.

It's a whole other world.

I lick her folds, and she cries out, her hands reaching to my head. Instead of pushing me away, she holds her hands there, clutching onto me as I chuckle.

I suck on either side of her pussy lips, taking my time, sucking, licking, nipping, then I pay attention to her clit. She bucks off the bed as I hold her down, her legs closing around my head. I don't give a fuck; I want to feel her come on my tongue.

Moving my fingers, I circle her hole as I insert a finger, making her gasp.

"Richie!"

"Are you close, baby?"

"Y-yes!"

"Do you like my mouth on your pussy, baby girl?"

"Don't stop!"

I grin, licking her clit as I insert another finger. I need her to come. I need to fuck her now.

Latching on, I suck her clit into my mouth and pump her pussy with my fingers, in and out, in and out… I feel her building, heat rising in her body as she stills, her knees finally letting go of my head as she comes, long and hard, calling out "Richie. Richie. Richie!"

When she's done, I cup her pussy as I move my body back over hers, kissing my way up her curves. My mouth finding hers, she gasps, tasting herself for the first time.

"I own this pussy," I tell her, my hand squeezing her there.

"Yes." She nods. "Yours."

I kiss her chastely, moving off the bed to find my jeans. Hunting around in my wallet, I pull out a rubber, rip the foil packet with my teeth, and roll it on deftly as she watches me.

"You should see how hot you look lyin' there like that," I growl, moving back over her.

To my surprise, she reaches for me, pulling me down on top of her as our lips crash together.

I hold my cock at the base and run the tip through her folds, sliding over her clit, her slickness coating me as I grip the sheets on either side of her head.

"Gonna let me in, baby girl?"

"Yes…" she cries when I swirl my tip over her clit once more, her hands digging into my ass. "Please…"

When she begs me, I could die a happy death.

I move the tip to her entrance. Feeling how slick she is makes me want to push into her fast, ruining her, taking her virginity, nailing her into the mattress.

But as she gazes up at me, a look of complete wonder and trust on her face, I know I can't do that.

I slide my tip in as she starts to breathe rapidly. I feel her walls constricting.

"Let me in," I tell her again. "It'll only hurt for a second. After that, it'll feel good."

She relaxes somewhat, her skin flushed, deliciously pink like her pussy.

I edge a little farther, my cock hard as can be as she sucks me in. I can already feel how tight she is. I'm not small and this is gonna hurt her, but I want it to feel good for her. Her first time is supposed to be great, not some dumb fuck nailing her for ten seconds and then it's all over. That would never be good enough for my girl.

I pull out, and when I push back in, I go even farther.

"Hutch!" she cries out. "Oh!"

"Shhh, baby," I say. "What's my name when I fuck you?"

"Oh…" She groans when I slide out again. "R-Richie."

I smile down at her. "Don't forget it," I say darkly, pushing all the way in.

She cries out as I still, seated to the hilt as she digs her nails into my ass.

Fuck, that's amazing. I've never been with a virgin before, but it feels so damn good.

Like every part of her is strangling my cock.

I may pass out from the sensation.

It takes all of my strength to not pull out and fuck her stupid. "You okay, Kirst?"

Her fingers let up as her eyes open, finding mine. "I'm perfect, Richie. Oh, wow, you're big."

I chuckle. "Yes, I am." I slide all the way out. "Can you feel how well your tight little pussy takes me, baby?" I slide back in slowly, knowing she feels every single inch of me. She winces, but nods rapidly. "How does it feel? Tell me."

I move slowly, in, out, in out.

"It feels…so good."

Kissing her quickly, I adjust onto my hands. "Wrap your legs around me." She does as she's told, and when I pull out next time, I slam back in harder.

"Oh!" she practically screams.

As I move my hips, I relish in every single murmur that comes out of her mouth. Her tits jiggle every time I thrust, and I can safely say; I've never, ever felt like this before.

Sex is usually fast.

I fuck hard.

I make sure she comes first; I'm not a total asshole, but I don't really take my time. I just get the job done.

With Kirsty, it could never be enough.

When her hands start to grip my ass harder again, I pump into her harder.

"Yeah, baby," I grunt, my orgasm building.

"Oh…oh…oh! Richie!" She comes, as I continue to thrust hard, my hands moving to clutch the headboard. I planned on adjusting her to ride me, but that ain't gonna happen this round. I'm too far gone.

"Kirsty…" I yell back, my seed shooting out of me violently. "Fuck!" I come hard, stilling as I empty myself into the rubber, wishing there was nothing between us.

I collapse on top of her as we both pant. I bury my face in her hair that smells like strawberries, and her legs loosen around me.

Still inside her I whisper. "You did good, baby girl. So, so good."

She groans, panting as she tries to catch her breath.

"Did I hurt you?" I lift off, concerned I was too rough.

She shakes her head, her skin glowing, eyes shining, her smile spreading across her face. She looks…happy. I smile back because it's contagious.

"That was…amazing, Hutch."

"Yeah?"

She nods.

When I pull out slowly, she winces. I take the rubber off, noting it's coated in a small amount of blood and throw it in the trash. I go to her bathroom and locate a washcloth, dampen it, and come back to the bed.

"What are you doing?" she breathes, sitting up, covering her tits again with her arms.

"Cleanin' you up."

It could be me, but her eyes glass over.

"Really?"

I frown, then my smile gets the better of me. "You gonna accuse me of bein' a nice guy again?"

She shakes her head. "No, but that is kinda sweet."

I lean down and kiss her as I place the cloth between her legs. "Let me do it."

I know this is hard for her, being naked in front of me, but she's got nothing to worry about. I wish she'd stop fuckin' hiding from me.

Tossing the cloth in the sink a few moments later, I come back to bed.

She rolls on her side, wrapping herself in her duvet.

I immediately pull it down so I can see her tits.

"I told you not to hide from me."

"I wasn't…"

I brush the hair back from her face. "What are you doin' to me, Kirsty Mason?"

She blinks a few times, as if trying to understand. "What are you doing to me, Richie Hutchison?"

I grin. "Give me some sugar."

She leans down, and my tongue finds hers as we kiss for a long time, then she squeals when I pull her on top of me. I'm hard again. One time was never gonna be enough.

Not with her.

My queen.

For the first time in a long time, I feel happy.

And I wanna bathe in that shit.

"Happy birthday, baby girl."

Hutch

BRACKEN RIDGE
REBELS
ARIZONA
M · C

CHAPTER 13

HIASTY

Hutch hisses as I take him into my mouth.

We've been at it all night. Touching each other, exploring, sucking, pulling, loving.

I know it's not love, not really, but I can pretend.

He's so tender.

Then he's rough.

And I like all of it.

He shows me what to do, how to hold him, how much pressure to use, and I lap it all up.

My tongue swirls around his salty tip as he sits spread-eagled, his back against the headboard as his hooded eyes watch me.

"Those lips…" he mutters. "Fuck, baby girl."

When he calls me that, I want to be his baby girl. I want to be his everything.

I know I'm falling and that it's stupid. I don't know what we are after tonight, but this…this is just fantastic. I can't get enough of him or his dick.

I take more of him. One hand reaches into my hair as he gently massages my head. He doesn't shove my head down or hold me there, he just coaxes. And I love every second of learning how to suck him off.

The noises he makes…I can feel myself dripping once again.

The sight and feel of him with his head between my legs…I thought I was going to have a heart attack. I'm sure most people's first times are not supposed to be like this.

With a guy who's experienced and knows what to do. In fact, I'd guarantee they're not.

I got lucky.

And I want to do a good job.

"Play with my balls," he says through gritted teeth.

I use my other hand to cup him gently, fingering his sack as he starts to move his hips.

"Mmmm," I murmur, tasting some of his saltiness leak from his tip.

I glance up at him. He has his eyes closed, mouth slightly parted, and his breathing is deep and rapid. I think I'm doing a good job…he looks like he's enjoying it.

His eyes open and they meet mine. I don't look away.

"Baby," he whispers, stilling his movements. "I don't wanna fuck your mouth…I'll come too fast…"

I ignore him, taking him deeper until I gag, almost choking as he pulls out.

His eyes crinkled with humor as he wags a finger at me. "Greedy girl."

I smile. "I love it."

"Love what, Kirst?"

He likes it when I tell him explicitly what I like. We've gone over all the dirty words.

I feel like such a bad girl when I use them, but I tingle all over when I do.

"Your…cock, baby."

I added the baby bit.

He grins. I lick his tip like a lollipop, and he groans again, then he reaches down and yanks me up so I'm spread over his knee. "Ride me, baby girl. Bounce those big tits in my face."

"Condom," I gasp.

"Fuck." He reaches to the bedside table and grabs one in haste, handing it to me. "Put it on me."

I fumble, sitting on his lap as his erect cock bobs. I can't get the damn thing out and on faster. He guides me, helping me roll it down and pinch the top, then he holds onto my forearms as I climb aboard.

"Hold me at the base, then sink down." He barely gets the words out as I do as he says.

He watches where we're joined, hissing as I sink down, taking all of him until he's seated all the way. It feels good…but different. "Hold on to my shoulders and I'll lift your ass so you can ride my cock."

I close my eyes, as his dirty talk sends a shock wave right through me.

Gripping my ass, I lift off, then I sink back down, and we both groan. He fills me so full, so tight…it feels like he's everywhere.

"Again, baby."

I do it again, my nails digging into his shoulders as I gain more confidence. One of his hands leaves my ass to cup my breast, bringing it to his mouth. He sucks on my nipple, his other hand leaving my ass, then spanks it lightly.

I yelp, flushing as I stop my movements.

He looks up at me. "Do you like that?"

I swallow hard. My throat feels like I've been in a desert.

"I…I don't know," I say honestly.

"Bad girls get spanked when they wear sheer blouses and dick tease," he grunts as I pick up my pace again. He sucks my nipple, flicking and tugging as I start to come undone. "Do you like teasing my dick, Kirsty?"

I feel bold. Like I have him right where I want him, so I surprise myself and say, "Yes."

He smiles around my nipple, moving to the other one. Plucking it, he licks, laves, sucking as I bounce faster, feeling my orgasm start to build again.

"You do?"

"Yes."

He smacks my ass again. Pleasure pounds in my wet center.

I do like that.

"I've been a very bad girl, Richie."

He just about chokes on my breast as a grin spreads across his face.

"Have you?"

I nod, as I move faster. He moves his hands to my hips and starts to bounce me up and down faster, faster…our skin slaps together, the sound echoing off the walls.

"Y-yes."

"Come for me," he demands.

I throw my head back as my orgasm rips through my body. Richie holds me tight, pounding up into me as I come. Before I know it, I'm being flipped over, and he's behind me, his hands clutch onto the headboard as he presses his hips against my ass.

Squeezing my butt cheeks he runs his fingers through my throbbing pussy, dipping them inside as he groans. I reach back, pulling his head to me as our lips join.

I'm unashamed as our tongues collide and our mouths replicate what we just did.

Pulling back, he mutters something incoherent, smacks my butt cheek again, then tells me to grip the headboard before shoving his dick inside of me as I hang on for dear life.

He pounds into me from behind, gripping my ass as he spreads my cheeks, whispering dirty, disgusting things in my ear that I can't get enough of.

"Kirsty," he groans. "Gonna come…can't hold on…"

I stick my ass out more as he pulls me back, one arm around my waist and the other gripping my breast, squeezing it hard as I hit another peak, my climax taking hold of me and sucking me under. I wail, not caring what I sound like or who hears me.

Two seconds later, he's calling my name over and over as he stills, holding me at the hips as he empties his seed inside me. I want so much for there to be nothing between us.

When we still, he's out of breath, and a small wash of pride comes over me.

Damn it. I did this. I made Richie Hutchison a freaking mess.

I start to giggle.

He kisses me on the shoulder, then pulls out. I slide back down on the bed as he discards the rubber, then he folds the duvet over and climbs in, pulling me with him.

"What's so funny?"

"Nothing," I say, as he wraps his arms around me.

"You shouldn't laugh after a man fucks you into oblivion," he replies, his tone laced with humor. "He might get a complex."

I snort. "You get a complex? I don't see that happening."

He chuckles softly, kissing the top of my head. Out of nowhere, he asks, "You sore?"

"Yes," I answer truthfully.

"Good. That'll remind you where I've been."

"I guess it will."

My heart beats rapidly, daring to believe he may want more.

He shifts and my stomach drops. I guess this is the part when he leaves.

At least he didn't leave after the first time, or the second…

Then, everything goes dark as he clicks off the lamp.

"Uh, what are you doing?" I ask after a moment of silence as he snuggles in behind me.

"Goin' to sleep, what does it look like?"

I find myself wondering something as I smile, my back to him as I take a breath. "Do you sleep with all the women you bang?"

"Bang?" he kisses my shoulder.

"You just don't seem like the snuggling kind."

"What's this then?"

"That's because you like me."

He chuckles. "Do I?"

"Yes, or you wouldn't be staying."

"Any other words of wisdom, or can I get some shut-eye?"

"I want to know."

"If I sleep with all the women I…bang?"

"Yes."

He sighs. "You know the answer to that."

"No, I don't."

"You know, I don't usually indulge in chatter after a bang-a-thon," he says, making me laugh. "But you're surprising the shit outta me right now, baby girl."

"You still didn't answer."

He bucks into me from behind. "No, I don't usually sleep with the women I bang. My bed is for sex and only sex. Happy now?"

Very, but I don't tell him that. "But this is my bed."

"Kirsty," he warns.

I bask in his warmth as he holds me tighter.

I'm falling for him. I know I shouldn't.

And after what he just did and the sensual assault he put on my body, I'm afraid I'll never be able to get enough of him.

"I can hear the cogs in your brain workin'," he mumbles, his voice sounding weary.

"Out with it."

"I know this is just sex…that we've only got tonight," I stammer. "But this was the best night of my life, Hutch…it was amazing…"

"Happy to be of service."

I shake my head, exasperated with him. Two seconds later, his breathing is slow and steady, and I realize he's fallen asleep.

I don't want my heart to dance.

I don't want my heart to feel happy.

And I especially don't want my heart to start having feelings.

I know what he's all about.

He still runs with a notorious and nasty motorcycle club. From the glimpse I got tonight, and judging by Hutch's reaction to me being there, I know it's not a place I really want to hang out.

I like how protective he is, even if he did headbutt the other biker before anything bad really even happened.

I was shocked at the violence, but clearly not shocked enough to let it deter me.

I close my eyes, not knowing what tomorrow will bring, and I find a part of me doesn't care.

As long as I'm with him.

And that is a very dangerous thought.

BRACKEN RIDGE
REBELS
ARIZONA
M · C

CHAPTER 14

HUTCH
TWO WEEKS LATER

I've kept her a secret.

I don't want my club brothers knowing about her. I made out that I punched Spyder because I wanted her first. He was so drunk he barely remembers anyway.

She's too pure for the Bracken Ridge Demons and though it goes against club ethics, not that we even have any, I won't share her, and she's not ready to be claimed. Claimin' her at nineteen…I gotta ask myself what the fuck I think I'm doing. She's got the whole world at her feet. She could do anything.

She can do better than me.

I've never had unrealistic expectations when it comes to women. It's always been easy, and that's not boasting, it's just the truth.

And if I tried to explain why I'm feeling this way, or what this feeling even is, I couldn't.

I just know how I feel when I'm around her. I'm itching

to see her every moment of the day.

I want to hear her voice.

I want to know what she thinks.

After our first time together, we've been inseparable. I've been going to her place every night. I can't get enough of her, and it's safe to say, she seems to feel the same way.

I know she's worried about her parents finding out, even if she hasn't even seen them and they seem to have washed their hands of her since she moved out after standing up to her mom.

She's told me a little here and there, about her mom putting her down and favoring her older sister and it makes me sad for her. She's clearly not the type of girl who would have given her parents a lick of trouble growing up.

The thought I'm corrupting her and leading her down a dark path consumes me. I don't want that. But I do want her.

The sweet butts at the club are starting to notice I'm not screwing around with any of them lately. It'll only be a matter of time before someone finds out.

Spyder was fishing around for more information about what happened that night, but I didn't give him shit.

He's lucky I didn't break his goddamn nose. It would've been worth it.

I could've just fucked Kirsty and been done with it, but let's face it; I'd gone way past go before we even slept together, another anomaly that I can't quite figure out.

It makes no sense.

I barely know her. I told myself so many times I should just walk away, but a selfish part of me wants to know more about her. I want to push the boundaries even further, even when I know it's wrong.

Does that make me a bad person?

I guess it doesn't make me a good one.

The next time I see Kirsty, though, I don't expect everything will come out in the wash, and we'll be outed, but that's exactly what happened. If it were my club, I doubt they'd care; they might even pat me on the back for keeping her away from club business until she can be trusted and I claim her. Or, they may even go as far to give me a beating for keeping secrets, but I don't give a shit. They can try.

But, as I'm heading up the stairs of the Stone Crow toward her apartment, I hear the voices of her parents on the landing.

"We just don't think that this is…you," her mom is saying as I hang back to listen, wondering if I should just turn back around and let them have privacy. "We're here to say that we're willing to have you back home again, but not under these conditions. I personally don't see how you could want this, Kirsty. This place is disgusting and unsafe. You've proven your point, and now you need to stop all this silly nonsense."

Her mom sounds like a snob, but I guess I figured that

one out from what Kirsty has already told me about her.

I think the time for being concerned about her kid should have come a long time ago.

"Mom, I don't want to come back. I'm happier here. I'm sorry you can't accept that, but it's the truth. I wouldn't ever stay somewhere that feels unsafe. Steph is lovely, and nobody has access up here. I like it." Nobody has access, except me, that is.

Her mom snorts. "Happier here? Living above a pub? Have you completely lost control of your senses, girl? John, will you say something to her?"

I can just imagine her mom's nose turned in the air as she looks down at her daughter with judgy eyes.

"Your mother's right," I hear her father say. "We were willing to overlook your past behavior, despite getting no apology, but this has to end, Kirsty. Our daughter can't be seen coming in and out of this place…it's a biker bar! I just don't even know what to say anymore. This isn't like you. Are you taking drugs?"

I slap a hand over my mouth. I hear Kirsty gasp at her father's words. I know this will hurt her. Despite her parent's behavior, she loves them.

Also, it isn't a biker bar, though some of the brothers do drink here, Steph doesn't put up with any shit. We established ground rules a while back, so the club doesn't terrorize the good folks of Bracken Ridge.

My little spitfire has come a long way in the short time I've known her. I know the time has to come when she stands up for herself, and I hope like hell now is that moment.

"I can't believe you just said that," Kirsty says, sounding defeated. "That you think…that you really think I'm taking drugs?"

"It would explain a lot," her mom agrees. "And you've lost weight." Her tone is so accusatory.

I don't think Kirsty has lost weight, and I wouldn't care if she did. The fact is, she's not wearing big, baggy clothes that cover up her beautiful body anymore. So maybe that's what her mom doesn't see. What the hell is this woman's problem?

"That should make you happier," Kirsty fires back. "Since I've been 'overweight,' according to you, since I hit puberty."

Her mom tuts. "What is that supposed to mean? I've never said that you're overweight, you're twisting my words around!"

"Right, like the watercress diet is because I need all those nourishing vitamins and minerals in my body. It has nothing to do with the fact you think I'm fat."

"This is not becoming of a well-bred girl like you who's had everything given to her."

"Mom, I'm paying my own tuition because you didn't

agree with my life choices. So I don't see how putting a roof over my head, feeding and clothing me is giving everything to me. Those are basically necessities that you took on when you became a parent, or more importantly because I thought you loved me. I'm grateful for what you've given me, but I'm not going to stand here while you both accuse me of taking drugs and being a bad person. I'm not a bad person. I don't know why you don't see that."

"This isn't how we raised you," her mom goes on, disapproval lacing her tone as she tries a different tact. "You're acting childish, Kirsty. I want you to pack your things and come on home before you get a reputation."

I can almost hear her blood boiling at that comment. As if it couldn't get any worse. "A reputation for what?" Kirsty demands.

"People talk," her father goes on. "It's a small town. Once your name is mud, Kirsty, no one will respect you."

I feel furious for her, hearing all these things getting thrown her way while she stands there and defends herself. If I go rushing up there, I'll blow our cover, and I don't want to land her in even more shit.

I know she wants to fight her battles with them on her own. As foreign as that feels to me, I'll bite my tongue for the moment, but listening to this horseshit is killing me.

"I don't care what strangers think of me," she replies. "I'm doing things my way from now on. I'm sorry that you can't respect my decision and the first conclusion you come to is I must be on drugs."

There're a few moments of awkward silence. "Your sister…"

"Please, Mom, just don't."

"I was going to say, your sister is coming down this weekend. It would be nice for you two to catch up and spend some time together."

"Why?" Kirsty fires back. "So she can tell me what a fat loser I am, like she does every time I see her? No thanks, I'd rather swallow shards of glass. The last time she was home, she made life pretty unbearable for me."

I don't know what she's referring to, but I'm guessing it ain't good.

"What a horrible thing to say! Your sister only wants what's best for you," her mom replies. "You just use any excuse to fight with her. The only one who is making life unbearable, Kirsty, is yourself."

Kirsty takes half a beat, but her words come out in a shitstorm. "I thought the worst thing I could ever hear out of your mouth is how disappointed you are in me and that you think I'm on drugs, but to hear that you think I purposely fight with my sister, even though she goes out of her way to be horrible to me, takes the cake. The fact that you don't see it and never will is even more disturbing. I'm not even sorry I can't be the daughter you really wanted. This is who I am.

I'm embracing it, as well as the career I'm carving out for myself. It's you that will miss out on being in my life, and that's the saddest part of all."

"Don't talk to your mother like that," her dad says, and I can just imagine him wagging a finger in her face. "She wants what's best for you, we both do."

"No, you want to control my life. I'm not going back to college, and I'm not coming home."

Woah, college? What's this?

Kirsty told me that she dropped out of college to enroll in business school, and then she scored an internship. Her parents had high hopes for her to be a lawyer or some shit, but she didn't want that.

"This conversation is pointless," her mom says, exasperated. "At least your sister is doing something with her life! What are you going to amount to, working in an office? Where could you possibly go from there?"

"I want to be a real estate agent," Kirsty says, a spark of confidence in her tone.

That's my girl. Here she comes.

Her mom laughs. It's a horrible, mocking sound. I don't hit women, but I want to slap the bitch.

"A real estate agent?" She scoffs. "Kirsty, have you lost your mind? You can't make a living from that."

Nope, her mind is sharp, pure, and fucking beautiful.

I love that she's smart; she's the whole goddamn

package. The longer I stand here listening, the more I want to go up there and smack her parents heads together.

Fuck them. She's done nothing wrong. She deserves so much better from her own flesh and blood.

"Why can't you just be happy for me?" Kirsty fires back. "Why do you always look down on me like it's a joke? Like I'm a joke?"

"You're being dramatic, Kirsty, and stand up straight!"

One more fucking word…

"This is exactly why I won't come home," she says. I can feel the heat rising in her as her tone gets higher. "I can't. I owe it to myself to see what I can become by myself, and thank you for asking, but I'm happy. For the first time in a long time, I'm actually happy."

"Kirsty…" Her dad, at least, sounds a little contrite.

"She's being dramatic," her mom counters. "That's all this is, rebellion, because we're such bad parents."

"I never said that."

"You didn't have to," she scoffs. "Your actions speak louder than words. You're punishing us, just admit it."

"I'm not admitting to any such thing," Kirsty says, her voice getting louder. "I want you to go now."

"No," her mom says. "We're not done yet!"

"Enough," her father says, and it sounds like there's a struggle. "This has to stop."

I can't wait any longer. I tear up the stairs two by two

until I'm on the landing, and Kirsty's eyes are wide as she stares at me.

Her dad turns to face me. "Who the hell are you?"

Kirsty clears her throat. "This is Hutch, he's my…"

"Friend," I butt in. "I heard yelling and came to check Kirsty was all right."

This is the first time I've seen her mom, and she's nothing like Kirsty. She's a slight thing, tall, and has curled, auburn hair. She is immaculately dressed like she's going to church.

Luckily, her dad doesn't seem to remember me from his shop that day, but they both stare at the patch on my cut.

"So much for this not being a biker bar," her mom comments, looking thoroughly disgusted. "Come on, John, let's go."

She pushes past me, indignance oozing off her as her father eyes me, passing me on the landing.

Thank fuck they're gone.

I turn to Kirsty and she's staring at me with wide eyes, tears forming.

"Baby girl," I say, going toward her.

"No!" she says, halting me in my tracks. "Just a friend, huh?"

"That's not what I meant."

Tears flow freely now. "Leave me alone, Hutch. I can't take any more heartbreak in one day. This is more than I can handle."

She turns, slamming the door in my face as I stare, stunned at the dramatic turn this took very quickly. And the worst part is, I don't know what the fuck to do to fix it.

BRACKEN RIDGE
REBELS
ARIZONA
M · C

CHAPTER 15

HIBSTY

How could he say that?

A friend?

I get my feelings are all over the place at the moment, but hearing him say I was just a friend sent me over the edge. Stupidly, I thought I was more to him.

Was he just using me all along? Because he's embarrassed to be seen with me? Because I'm so wretched that he didn't even want my parents to know we're a thing?

He won't even allow me into his own clubhouse. He obviously doesn't want people knowing he's seeing who he's currently screwing.

Am I really nothing to him?

All I know is we fuck, a lot, and he likes it as much as I do, but there's been no real talk about what we are or where we're going. Is he even my boyfriend?

Or am I just some lame chick who let him take my virginity while I defy my parents and try to navigate myself through this maze alone.

I've never felt more alone in my life.

I slump back against my door as Hutch bangs on the other side of it.

"Kirsty!" he pleads. "Let me in. I didn't mean that…I didn't want to get you in any more trouble with your parents."

It's a lie. Like my entire life is a lie.

My own parents think I'm taking drugs. Imagine if they knew who Hutch really was and what we'd been up to. They'd probably put a restraining order on him and have me committed. The look on my mom's face…I've never been a violent person, but the way she treated me just now has made me snap. Looking down on me like I'm scum. Like she wonders where she went wrong. Like I'm some drop out.

I don't give a shit any more. About anything.

"Please, Kirsty, open this fucking door, now!"

"No!" I yell back. "Leave me alone, Hutch, I don't want to talk to you!"

"I don't want to fight through a fuckin' door!"

"Then go away!"

He bangs again, and I close my eyes.

Please, just go away. I can't do this anymore. I can't deal with my parents and this as well.

I knew my heart was getting involved the night he took my virginity. I knew it was stupid to fall for him. He doesn't care about me, not really. He just wants a warm bed to come home to and a vagina that hasn't slept with any other men in that awful clubhouse.

"I won't say it again," I cry out when his pounding doesn't let up. "I'll call the police!"

"Go right ahead, baby girl, see how far that gets you."

I move from the door and into the tiny room, trying to back as far away as possible.

I just need some time.

A few minutes go by as I sit on the end of my bed and sob quietly. Then, just when I think he's actually given up, I hear him at the door again.

"I won't give up on you, Kirsty," he says, his tone sharp and final. "I heard everything, and I wanted to tell you how proud I am of you for doing what you did. I didn't want to come up the stairs and get you in even more shit with your parents. You're more than a friend to me, you know that…I think…fuck…I don't even know how to say this…but…I think…I think I'm falling in love with you, baby girl."

I stop my blubbering.

What?

"You're all I think about, day and night. I want you with me. I want to show you to the world, tell everyone you're mine. I don't wanna sneak around anymore."

I part my lips to speak, but no sound comes out.

"So you take this time, Kirsty, take what you need, and when you're ready to take the leap with me and be my woman for good, come to the clubhouse and ask for me at the gate."

I curl my legs up underneath me and rest my chin on my knees. I don't know what to feel right now. Isn't this what I wanted?

"I love you, Kirsty. Come to the clubhouse. I don't want to hide anymore."

With one final thump of his fist on the door, I hear him leave, his heavy footsteps thudding down the stairs as he makes his retreat.

I sit there, stunned, unable to speak or move.

He loves me?

I know I love him too. So much that it hurts my heart when we're apart.

I've been holding all of this inside, unable to break free in fear that he wouldn't want me, or that this was just us fooling around and nothing more. I've safeguarded my feelings on the surface so deep down they don't wreck my entire being. I know that Hutch has the power to undo me, but without him, I don't honestly know what there is anymore. I want him.

I don't care what my parents say or do; they can't stop me now, not ever.

I finally stood up to them, and aside from the argument I just had with Hutch, it feels fantastic to get that all off my chest.

I can't forgive my parents for thinking I'm on drugs, that was the lowest of blows. I had never touched drugs in my life, and I don't plan on doing that now.

I know if they knew about Hutch and me, they'd have a coronary, but that's their problem, not mine.

Wiping my eyes, I take myself to the shower. A good, scalding hot wash while I think about what I'm going to do is just what I need.

Crying won't get me anywhere. I need to work out what I want, and if that's with Hutch, then I know it comes with being a part of that club.

I just don't know if I can do that. The biker gang thing scares me, but I'm open to what he has to say.

I have to be. I don't want to make a mistake and throw away what we have before he's even had the chance to talk. I owe him that much.

Lucky for me, I have class to distract me all the next day, and when I finally leave school, I know what decision I have made.

I can't stop thinking about him. About what we could be and what I want.

If it's a future with him, I need to know what that looks like.

I need to know what his plans are and what it means for me if he claims me as his woman.

I want to be Hutch's and nobody else's. I want to be the only woman in his arms because, rest assured, I won't be sharing him. If Hutch wants me, then he gets me exclusively, and the same goes for him.

I hurry home to change, knowing that I can't wait to see my man tonight.

I have so much to tell him, so much to say, because even though I know that my head is saying one thing, my heart is saying another.

I don't have a car, so I walk the few miles out of town to the clubhouse. I could have gotten a cab, but I needed the fresh air to think about what I'm doing and what this means.

If he wants me at the clubhouse, then this means he's serious. That I am someone important to him, not someone he chooses to keep as some dirty little secret.

By the time I arrive, I'm a little short on breath. I didn't realize that while I was walking and thinking, I practically jogged here.

I straighten myself out, take a couple of well needed deep breaths, and smooth my hair. I spent some time paying extra attention to my appearance, wearing jeans and a form-fitting top, with my faux leather jacket over the top. The jeans hug my curves and make me feel sexy, and they're the ones Hutch always comments on.

I feel alive tonight.

Yesterday, I was annoyed and overwhelmed and I took it out on him.

I really just thought he was another person in my life who didn't see me, or want to be seen with me. After the barrage from my parents, I just couldn't take any more.

When I ask for him at the gate, I'm giddy with excitement, but also nervous.

My palms start to sweat as I wait for what feels like an eternity for the gate to open.

The young man waiting, with the leather jacket on labeled "Prospect", tells me I'm free to go inside.

Nervously, I take a few steps past the gate, turning to look behind me, as if there are any other options for me back there. I know there aren't. This is where I belong, wherever Hutch is.

I don't even make it halfway down the driveway when I see that he's walking toward me, striding in long paces like his life depends on getting to me.

I start to run, because being away from him for even one night was enough to make me never want to be away from him again.

"You came," he says as I smack into his chest, and he lifts me off the ground and holds me tight, bringing his lips to mine as we kiss. "You fuckin' came."

"I love you, Richie," I say, as I try not to cry. "I'm

sorry…for shutting you out like that. I was just so mad at my parents, but I know that's no excuse…"

He sets me down on my feet, cupping my face, staring into my eyes like he can't believe I'm really here. I've never felt so loved.

"I don't care about that," he says, stroking my face with his thumbs as his lips curve into a smile. "The fact is, you're here. You're mine now. Whatever happens from here, we can deal with it together."

My heart gallops in my chest at his words.

"I want that so much, I really do."

His lips crush mine, and before I know it, he's backing me up into the nearest tree, lifting my legs as I wrap them around his waist.

"Don't ever shut me out again," he says between kisses. "I love you, Kirsty Mason. I loved you from the first moment you almost spilled my coffee."

I kiss him back with a fervour I've never felt before. Pain and pleasure rushing between my legs. "You're the one who almost spilled your coffee on me."

He chuckles. "Are we always gonna fight about this?"

"I hope not. I'd rather spend my time doing more productive things."

He raises any eyebrow. "Oh yeah? Such as?"

I reach between his legs and cup his hardness. He groans, biting down on his bottom lip as I squeeze.

"Playing with this."

"I want you to do more than play with it."

I laugh. "I want to make you happy," I say out of nowhere. "This is crazy…but around you, I feel so alive."

He smiles, his eyes crinkling at the corners. I know I will love this man forever.

The rest of my life, it will only be him. I know that now.

"I do too, which is why I didn't want you to shut me out. I know this is gonna be hard, Kirst. There's shit goin' on at the club that I can't involve you in or tell you about, but if you trust me, I have a plan."

I nod. "Okay."

"I'm not gonna be doin' all this illegal shit forever, baby, but for right now, I've gotta play the game. I've gotta get numbers on my side, and when Scar fucks up one too many times, I'm gonna be there, ready."

I look at him, wide-eyed. "You're going to be Prez?"

He chuckles, hearing me use club slang for the first time. "Oh yeah, baby. One day I am. Now, what I say to you is only to you, got me? Don't go raggin' me out to your girlfriends, because they talk to the other brothers and if that happens, I'm dead, do you understand?"

I nod furiously as I watch his dilemma. He runs a hand through the mop of hair that I love so much.

"Some of us in the club don't like where Scar is takin' things. We disagree on most things, but I'm not part of the committee yet, meanin', I don't get a vote. Some of the members do, though, and we're gonna stick together and try to get him out. After that, change will happen, baby girl. Skull will likely step up for a short time. But until then, I gotta try and keep my head above water."

"It doesn't matter, Hutch, if I'm with you."

He presses his body back to mine. Even for those few brief seconds, it felt cold without him. "I don't wanna keep shit from you, but with club business, I have to. It's for your own good that you don't know, but just know that I'm makin' changes, baby, for our future, because I want to be with you."

"Only me?" I say, not hearing anything else because I don't care. I should, but I don't.

"Only you."

I tug him by the lapels of his jacket. "I won't share you, Richie."

He smirks. "So it's Richie when I'm fuckin' you, and Richie when I'm in trouble?"

"That sounds about right."

He kisses me again, forcing his tongue into my mouth. We kiss for a long time. Wrapping my arms around his neck, he pushes his erection into the throbbing ache between my legs.

"You won't be sharin' me."

"Good, because it works both ways."

We're both talking in between kissing, our hands everywhere, our bodies heated and ready to burst.

"I have to claim you, at the table," he says. "So you're off limits to anyone else at the club. For your own protection, and my sanity."

"Okay."

"Agreeing so quickly?"

"I told you, I love you, Hutch. There's nobody else. I want you and all that comes with you. If you say you're making a change for the better, I believe you. I know you're a good man. You're kind, sweet, honest, and you have a good head on your shoulders. I just never want there to be any lies between us. I always want the truth."

"Even if I can't tell you everything to do with club business?"

"I know you won't put me in any immediate danger."

"That's just it, with the club as it is now, it's dangerous, baby girl. You'll have to be at the club, hang around, make friends with some of the ol' ladies. The sweet butts won't be happy…"

"Sweet butts?" I groan. "I really don't want to know."

"But it's all part of a plan. Do you think you can do that?"

I look up at him, my heart open and my mind reeling. "If it means I get you, Richie Hutchison, then yes, I can do it."

"I love you," he says, his lips pressing against mine once more. "I really fuckin' love you."

BRACKEN RIDGE
REBELS
ARIZONA
M · C

CHAPTER 16

HUTCH

ONE YEAR LATER

I stare at my woman from across the clubhouse. I've been away for a few days on club business, and I've been observing her without her knowledge for a few long moments.

It's hard to believe it's been a whole year since we came clean about us and then took things to the next level. When shit's been rough at the club, Kirsty is always there when I get home to make it all better. She listens without judgment, and over this last year, she's not only become my lover and the woman I can't get enough of, but she's my best friend and confidant.

I moved into her apartment not long after she came to the clubhouse. Much to her parents' dismay. They barely talk to her these days. I don't like the fact she's isolated from them, but they made it that way. If they treated her like a normal human being and like a daughter they're proud of, I'd have no issue at all going to family gatherings. But all they've done is push her further away.

I hate that for her. If I could do anything to change it, I would.

She spots me eyeing her up. Instantly, her eyes light up as she smiles. God, I love it when she looks at me like that. It's not just the come-fuck-me eyes, which I dig, it's how I know I'm the only man she's ever been with and will ever be with.

I wet my lips, giving her the same look back; the one she can't resist.

Kirsty has come so far in this last year, working through the second year of her internship and taking on her own listings at the real estate office. I'm proud of her.

She's fit in well enough at the club. We had issues with the sweet butts in the beginning, but that was to be expected. She made fast friends with the important women of the club and the ol' ladies. Who wouldn't fall in love with her?

Although, having claimed her at the table, that puts all the other brothers in the club on notice if they ever tried anything.

Back when we first declared our love for one another, I realized she was exactly like me in so many ways; scared of being loved. But when we both let our guards down, we knew that we were going to work. We'd defy the odds. I'll fight anyone who says any different.

I beckon her to me with the crook of my finger, but instead of coming to me, she shakes her head subtly.

I quirk an eyebrow. She knows better than that. I'm not a possessive man by nature, but I am protective. And when I want her to come to me, there is no question.

She rolls her lips, knowing she's testing me. My patience only goes so far, so when I crack my neck from side to side, she purses her lips into a smile and pushes off the bar.

That's my girl.

She swings those hips as she walks to me. She'll forever be my muse. The woman who I can't get enough of. The woman of my dreams. And she's mine.

"You dodgin' me, baby girl?" I say when she folds into my embrace, wrapping her arms around my neck as I grab her ass with one hand. She tries to slap my hand away, but I just grip harder.

"Never. I wanted to see if you'd come haul me off like a caveman."

"Don't give me ideas." My eyes drop to her soft, plump lips. "Give me some sugar."

She kisses me, pulling me in as I grip her ass harder. Our tongues meet and my cock hardens. Fuck, she smells good.

I groan, grinding her against my cock.

"Hutch," she gasps. "You're very happy to see me."

"I'm always happy to see you."

I cup her face with my spare hand and our kiss deepens.

When we pull back, she says, "I missed you."

It's like music to my ears. I want her to fuckin' miss me.

I've been keeping my promise, but it's slow going. We've had ups and downs with the club, but Scar recently got put in jail. The past finally caught up with him, and without him in the picture, the committee voted Skull in as the next Prez. Rainman moved to VP. And I moved up to Treasurer. It's not where I wanna be in the grand scheme of things, but the truth is, I get a vote now. I never wanted to go against my Prez, but he took one too many risks, putting the whole club in danger. I hope that Skull can turn things around. I'm close to being done with drugs and guns. Seen too many brothers go down or end up in a concrete box, just like Scar.

"Missed you too. Did you think of me?"

She smiles, pushing her body against mine, rubbing against my cock. "Mmhmm."

"Did you touch yourself?"

She bites her bottom lip. She does that purposely now, because she knows what it does to me. "You know the answer to that."

I pinch her ass as she squeals. "Hutch!"

"You know that pussy is mine."

She shakes her head. "Show me."

I smirk. "Right here?"

She rolls her eyes. We may be very racy in the bedroom these days, but we're not exhibitionists like some of the ol' ladies. I prefer to keep my woman's body all to myself.

Instead, she grabs my hand, hauls me off my perch against the wall, and tugs me toward the back room.

I don't have a spare room here anymore, and I definitely don't wanna fuck her on some prospect's dirty bed. So we head to the back room where the kegs are stored.

The second we're in there, I kick the door shut with my boot.

My eyes on her, she's already unbuttoning her tight blouse, her massive tits plump and suckable. My eyes lower, watching her movements as I start to unbuckle my belt.

I'm going straight in. We both need this.

"Take those big tits out," I tell her when her blouse is open at the nape.

She pulls her bra cups down and I stare at her tits as I undo my zipper.

"You get more beautiful every time I see you naked."

She smiles, beckoning me with her finger, trying to be a smart-ass.

When I reach her, I drop my jeans to my knees, my cock springing free. I grab her hand and place it on my cock, as my other hand reaches for her breast. I give it a squeeze, and she tilts her head back and moans.

I drop my head, sucking her nipple into my mouth as

she fists my dick, giving me exactly what I want because I taught her so well.

"Feel what you do to me?" I growl.

"Mmm," she replies as I cup her breast, suckling like a man who can never get enough. She grips my cock and starts to jerk me off, just how I like it.

"Fuck yeah."

"Don't leave me again," she purrs as I move my mouth to her other nipple, trying to stuff more of her in my mouth. "I hate it when you're gone."

I grow harder, precum leaking out. She knows what it does to me when she misses me. "I hate it when I'm gone."

I move my hands to the front of her jeans, undoing the button and fumbling with the zipper. When I finally get it down, I peel her jeans down her thighs, along with the G-string she has on, so small she may as well not be wearing it, and I growl some more. I bend down, pushing my face against her pussy as I inhale. Fuckin' perfect.

"You miss me, baby?"

"Oh, yes."

I smile. "Spread your legs."

"I need your cock, baby."

"And you'll get it, but I need some honey first." I wasn't planning this. I wanna fuck her hard and fast, but I need just a taste.

She does as I say, and I sheath myself as I spread her

pussy with one hand, licking through her folds as she gasps. She's soaking.

"Baby girl," I mumble as she moans, her hands reaching down into my hair. I wear it longer now, tied back into a ponytail. "So wet for me."

"Always," she mutters.

"Tell me."

"I want it."

"How badly?" I lick her again, from her hole to her clit, sucking on her pussy lips, one then the other as she cries out.

"So bad."

"Is that why your pussy's wet for me?"

"Oh, God…I want you, Richie."

I circle her clit with my tongue and spread her slickness around her hole as I ease two fingers inside. When I latch onto her clit, her hands grip my head and I bury my face.

I love this, making her come undone. Taking her exactly how I want to.

I like making the rules, but I sure as hell love it when she breaks them.

She comes hard and fast as I lap her up. Our eyes meet and I've never been so hard.

Standing, I yank her to me, her greedy little hand on my cock as she fists me again.

"You're a dirty little girl, aren't you? Lettin' me suck your pussy with your tits hangin' out." My lips are against hers, but I don't kiss her.

"Put your dick in me, baby, I need it."

Fuck. I love it when my nerdy, business-minded woman talks dirty to me. It's so hot.

"You want my big cock, baby girl?"

We also love to role play. Right now, she pretends to be a virgin.

Before that, a nurse. With a costume and everything.

"I'm scared it won't fit. I've never done this before."

Jesus, I almost come.

I kiss her hard, my tongue in her mouth as she groans, grinding against me as she tries to guide my cock to her entrance.

Smirking, I knock her hand away, spinning her around. I spank her ass once, twice.

"That's for wearin' those tight jeans." I smack her ass again, and she moans, sticking her ass out farther. She loves to be spanked, too. And man do I love it when her pale skin starts to turn pink. "And this is for not comin' to me when I told you the first time."

I bend her over farther, her arms resting on the kegs as I yank her hips back, lining my cock up to her juicy, pink hole.

"Get it inside me, please," she begs, wiggling her ass. She cups her tits and starts to pull her nipples. Goddamn it. I love nothing more than to watch her getting herself off.

But now it's my turn.

I spank her again, her ass cheeks turning a delicious shade of red as I smooth my palm immediately after I spank her. My mouth at her ear, I say, "What are you, baby girl?"

"Your dirty whore," she groans.

I spank her again.

"Try again."

"Your dirty little bitch."

I spank her pussy this time, and she just about convulses on my palm.

"Kirsty," I warn.

She pushes her ass back, almost mounting me as I line up my cock, so ready to fuck her hard. "Your queen."

I grin, grabbing her hips, and I shove into her balls deep. I don't let her adjust; she's got me into this state, she can deal with it. I pull out, then slam back in again.

She cries out, and I fist her hair with one hand, pulling her head back as I suck on her neck.

"You're my queen. Say it again."

"I'm your queen," she cries.

I slam in, and then pull out again, her pussy taking me so damn good.

"Good. Now don't forget it. Hold on."

I slam back in and then start to fuck her hard, in out, in out, my hands digging into her hips as she hangs onto the kegs, her tits bouncing over the top of them as our skin slaps together.

"When will you let me put babies in you?" I groan.

We've had this conversation too. I never thought I wanted kids until I met her. Now I want a bunch of them. I know she has things she wants to do with her career, and I respect that, but I still like reminding her that when she's ready, I'm ready too.

"Soon."

I plunge in and out, gripping one ass cheek as she bounces back and forth on my dick. Getting herself off, taking what she wants. My good girl.

Her body is so curvy, so soft and warm. I can't get enough of her ass, her tits, her stomach; every single part of her that she used to hate, she's now learned to love. I kiss every inch of her body every chance I get, to remind her how beautiful she is.

"Fuck, baby, gonna come. It's gonna be quick."

"I want your cum inside me, Richie, please. Harder, baby."

That sets me off as she climaxes, crying out as I pump her harder, faster, my cum shooting out as I still, gripping her hips again, filling her full as I see stars from the intensity.

When we're done, I stay inside her as she slumps forward, gasping for air.

I kiss her neck, sucking on her skin until I know I'll

leave a mark. Just like I always do. I like her to look in the mirror and see it, reminding her of who she belongs to. "I should go away more often," I muse, kissing her hair.

"Shut up and get me home. I need to do that again, except this time I want your cock down my throat."

There are no sweeter words for a man who's missed his woman to hear. I could live like this forever.

"Now that I can do, baby girl."

BRACKEN RIDGE
REBELS
ARIZONA
M · C

CHAPTER 17

KIRSTY

FIVE YEARS LATER

I stare at the pregnancy stick, my heart palpitating as I will the lines to appear.

Two blue.

Two blue.

I want this so bad.

I've wanted it bad the other three times, but I've already had two miscarriages early on and one false alarm. The doctors say I'm at high risk should another miscarriage occur, and they've put it down to an abnormality in my uterus, called uterine septum. I underwent a hysteroscopy, and after an examination of the uterus, I had surgery to repair the tissue band. I'm hoping that will mean I can carry our baby without any problems this time, should the test be positive.

We both want this so much. I'm twenty-five now, and I want to have kids before I'm thirty.

I've done the research, and while the odds of miscarrying again are high, a large percentage of women conceive perfectly fine after this kind of surgery. I'm hopeful.

We've been so disappointed these last few years of trying, then the excitement of being pregnant, only to lose the baby before I even got through the first trimester.

This time it feels different. It feels good.

I hope it's not just wishful thinking, but I've been doing all the right things. Nourishing my body, staying away from the cigarette smoke at the clubhouse, not drinking, getting enough sleep, and keeping my weight the same without fluctuating too much.

And we've been practicing like rabbits.

We've been together for over six years now, and Hutch's hunger for me hasn't expired. If anything, it's gotten even more intense.

The more I think about him and the way he looks at me, the more I want to be barefoot and pregnant, being a good ol' lady and taking care of him. Just as he takes care of me.

Life is good, and it's getting better every day.

We bought a house. It's small, and on the outskirts of town, but it's a home we can grow into when we have kids. I'm a partner now in Bracken Ridge Real Estate. Hutch wants to buy more property. After I showed him a projection of what I predict things will be worth in another five-to-ten years' time, he's on board with all of it.

Now is the time to buy. Bracken Ridge is a beautiful town with beautiful people. The draw card is its uniqueness;

it's vibrant and bustling without the big price tag of a major city. There is room for businesses and more housing to develop, and I know of several new land releases coming up in the next year or two. I'm putting a bid in with the firm to the developers so we can have full exclusivity. There're two other real estate offices in town, but we're fiercely competitive, and I love what I do.

And as for Bracken Ridge, we both love it here.

I sit on the toilet seat with the lid down, unable to breathe.

Richie is VP now. He loves this club. Even though Skull has changed a lot of the club antics, he still refuses to go vanilla. And I've looked the other way for a long time.

Shit's getting riskier. The drugs are getting nastier. I know that Hutch and I both want the same thing, and Hutch has worked so hard to be one of the forces in turning this club around. He was right about it taking time, as change always does. Old people go and new people come in, the dynamics always evolving.

But I know they have a big drop going down soon, one that'll line their pockets one last time, and Hutch has a bad feeling about it.

Just like he has all the other times when shit went wrong. I trust his judgment, and I know how hard it is for him to go against his Prez at the table. He rarely does. Most of the time, the votes are in Skull's favor, but this time,

Hutch being so worried scares me.

I close my eyes.

Maybe if those two blue lines appear, Hutch will reconsider the drop. He'll understand that things are different now.

I'm terrified he'll go to jail, or worse. The latter, I can't even think about. I won't go there. I love him too much. We've come so far in six years. I couldn't bear anything to happen that separates us. But, the fact remains; the club has lost a lot of brothers over the years, either fighting it out with nearby rival clubs, being shot or mysteriously going missing, or drug deals gone wrong and the feds swooping in.

This is a dangerous game and I live on tenterhooks that nothing happens to Hutch and the members who have been good to him, to us.

My parents were right, I did get a reputation, but I try to not think about that too much. Mud sticks in a small town. No matter if the club was or wasn't a one-percent organization, people would still talk and think the worst of you.

I don't agree with the bad shit they do. I can't even bear to think about where these drugs end up and whose hands the guns land in. It's too scary to think about.

Once Hutch is Prez, everything will change. There is no doubt in my mind it'll happen, but I just hope it happens sooner rather than later.

I glance down at the stick.

Two blue lines.

I jump up, running to the window to test it in the daylight, just to make sure. Holy shit.

I skipped a period, so I was pretty confident something was going on. To be sure, I take a second test, and I get the same result.

I immediately grab the phone and dial the doctor, making an appointment to have a proper pregnancy test. I don't want to alert Hutch until it's confirmed.

Things feel different this time.

Hugging myself, I think about our baby growing inside me, and I get emotional, tears leaking from my eyes as I take a few deep breaths to steady myself.

I want this more than anything in the world.

I want a baby of my own.

I want to give Hutch this very special gift. One that we both want. One that would be like a miracle after what we've endured.

Just once I want things to go right.

I put my hand on my stomach. "It's okay, little bump, we're gonna be okay this time."

I hope to God I'm right.

This baby is our miracle.

We both want it so badly. In fact, I've never wanted anything more in my whole life.

To be the mother of his kids, it's a dream.

The doctor confirms I'm almost three weeks pregnant. I know we've been down this road before, and I shouldn't get my hopes up until we're past the first trimester, but I can't help but have a spring in my step as I rush to the supermarket to make Hutch's favorite meal so I can give him the good news when he gets home.

I busy myself, taking my time because I want this to be special. When he gets home before nightfall, he looks weary as he comes into the kitchen, already having kicked off his boots in the hallway.

He comes over to me and kisses me. "Mmm, something smells good."

I kiss him back, deepening it further when his hands come to my apron, and he grips my hips.

"How was everything at the club?" I try to change the subject, but I know I can't hide the smile on my face.

"Good. Why are you so chipper?" He stands back, assessing me as I fiddle with the buttons on his shirt.

"Can't I just be happy to see you?"

He pulls my apron string loose at the back, sliding his hands under as he cups my breasts. I'm a little tender, and wincing, he frowns. "Baby girl?"

"Yes?"

"You're makin' my favorite meal, you're beamin' from

here to Timbuktu, and your tits are sore? What's goin' on?"

I swing my arms around his neck, my bottom lip trembling as he stares at me. "I'm pregnant, Richie Hutchison."

He blinks once, twice, then a grin spreads across his face. "You're serious?"

I nod. "I took two tests, then I went to the doctor and they confirmed it. Three weeks."

He pulls me to him, his eyes glazing over as he kisses me chastely, then hugs me tight. "Fuck, baby, you had me worried there for a second. I'm so fuckin' happy."

"You are?"

He pulls back. "Of course I am! Why would I not be?"

I shake my head. "After the last few times…"

He cups my face. "That was then, this is now. It's gonna be okay this time, baby girl." His hands come to my stomach, where he places his palms there, looking down as if he'll see some sign of my big belly. Of course there isn't.

"I know, I just worry…"

"You know what the doc said about worrying. You're to de-stress, which is why I don't want you workin' until you get past this first hurdle."

"But, Hutch," I start to protest.

He places a finger over my lips. "No buts. I don't want no wife of mine to be workin' while carryin' my kid."

"But I'm not your wife." I swallow hard. I'll do

anything he says; I'll slow down at work until I get the all-clear. I don't want to do anything to jeopardize this chance.

"You will be. I wanna marry you. Now. Today. Tomorrow. Let's not wait."

"But we can't. We'd have to plan it." I've always dreamed of marrying Hutch, but I don't honestly know what that would look like.

"Get some of the girls together. We'll get married at the registers, and we'll have a party at the clubhouse."

"I love you so fucking much," I breathe.

He smiles, cupping my ass as he presses his cock into me, and I shake my head. "I'm gonna be a daddy."

"It's that thing that got us into this mess in the first place," I muse.

He kisses me again. "I can't wait for this belly to grow. You're gonna look so fuckin' sexy with my kid inside you." He lifts me in the air, holding me as he looks up, his smile spread across his face. I love making him happy.

"I want this so much," I say, when he brings me back down and I fold into his arms. "I want so much to give you this."

He kisses the top of my hair. "I know, baby, I know."

I deepen the kiss, but he pulls back. I frown. "Hutch?"

He shakes his head. "We don't wanna risk anythin'…"

I take a deep breath. "The doctor said we can still have sex. It's fine, nothing bad will happen."

He frowns. "I don't know. I don't think it's a good idea."

I reach between his legs and cup his hard dick. "It feels like a good idea to me."

"Kirsty," he warns.

I knew this was going to be an issue, as he was like this the last time, before I miscarried. At first, I thought it was me, that he didn't want to touch me at all, but when we talked about it, I learned it was because he didn't want to ruin our chances. I had to get the doctor to explain that it wouldn't.

"I'm so horny, baby," I purr, nibbling at his neck while his hands cup my ass. "Or should I say, daddy."

"Fuck, Kirst."

"Hmm." I kiss his pulse point, biting gently as I massage his cock. "Daddy, yes, it has a certain ring to it."

He hauls me up, sitting me on the bench while he rips my apron off, and then shreds my dress apart. The buttons go flying everywhere as I laugh, pulling his cut off as it slides off his shoulders and hits the ground.

"I love you so much, mama," he growls the last part as I pull him closer, reaching for his buckle.

"Say that again when you're inside me," I beg. "I love you so damn much."

BRACKEN RIDGE
REBELS
ARIZONA
M · C

CHAPTER 10

HUTCH
THREE MONTHS LATER

This doesn't feel right.

Just like the last time, I remind myself. Just like the same shitty club business that I'm sick of. Nobody would listen then, and I doubt they will now.

It's too risky. And I got a tip-off from a reliable source that the dealer we're doing business with is shady.

I've made my reservations clear to Skull, but he's made up his mind. And the committee has the majority vote. It doesn't matter that half the members, who don't get a say, disagree too. Even if I do have Harlem on my side, Skull wants the pay dirt.

The one that'll line our pockets so we can steer away from drug dealing. This one last time. Just like the last time.

I run a hand through my hair. Every fiber of my being tells me this is a bad idea.

We're friends, he's a good guy. But he's getting greedy. We're all older now, we've got families, and I've got a kid on the way.

Kirsty is past her first trimester and the baby growing inside her belly is healthy. I've never felt such a wave of relief hearing those words from the doc's mouth.

Our baby.

He or she is a miracle and is wanted more than anything. Kirsty's gonna get through this and be a mother, and I'm gonna be a father. Like we always wanted. I couldn't be any happier right now, yet this dread washes over me.

And not for the first time.

For weeks, I've been wrestling with my decision on what to do with this drop. And I'm no closer to finding an answer, one I'm happy with.

On the one hand, I defy my Prez and potentially lose respect within the ranks, maybe even get voted out. Yet on the other, the members who don't agree with what's going down will form an alliance. That could be good if the shit really hits the fan. Not that I want Skull out, nor do I want anarchy, but we all know this is the most drugs to ever change hands in the history of the club, and the bigger the drop, the riskier it is.

I know for a fact through an informant that the Feds could be watching. If that happens, we're all dead.

The drop is supposed to go down in two days time.

As I crawl into bed, my wife stirs. Turning to look over

her shoulder, she murmurs.

"Go back to sleep, baby girl," I say softly, snuggling in behind her.

"Is everything okay?" Kirsty never asks: what's wrong? It only opens a whole can of worms that I'm not gonna share.

I've kept club business away from Kirsty as much as humanly possible. She knows the drill, and she knows the respect I've gained over the years and the way things are moving in the right direction. I don't wanna give up on this club, not ever, but Skull seems hell-bent on greed and nothing more. It's what almost ruined the club back when Scar was Prez, and he's serving twenty years to life in maximum security.

I let out a deep sigh.

"Baby?" she goes on when I don't answer.

"Everythin's fine," I tell her, wrapping my arms around her body. My hands cup her swollen belly. "Did I tell you today that I love you?" I kiss her hair.

"Not as much as I love you."

I swallow hard. "What if I'm not a good father?"

She stiffens in my arms. "What are you talking about? You're gonna be a great father."

"But what if I don't do it right?"

She shifts in my arms, trying to turn. "Help," she says as I chuckle.

I help her sit up, and she turns to face me. "I don't want you worryin' about this," I say. "I shouldn't bug you with this shit."

She cups my face as I stare at her. "Don't ever say that. We're in this together." She pauses. "Hutch, what's wrong?"

"You know what. The same shit, as always."

"So, tell Skull how you feel."

"I did, he won't listen."

"Did you vote?"

"Yes. And he got the majority. Doesn't mean everyone is happy about it."

"Then you have to decide."

"There's so much to lose." I rub her stomach, feeling the warmth of her belly.

I think about the argument Skull and I had.

I've gone along with a lot of shit over the years, and I've felt guilty about a lot of bad stuff that went down. Now I've got a kid on the way, things feel different.

I don't want my kid out there on the street, taking the shit we sell and it fucking them up. I close my eyes, the pain in my head not going away.

I know what I have to do, and that's what makes it worse.

If I go against my Prez, they'll strip me of my colors. I'll be banished from the club. I'll probably get my ass kicked - well, they can try. I don't know because nobody has ever said no before. But when is enough, enough?

"Then you know what you have to do," she says. "You always have."

"I never wanted to be a traitor."

"If you know something's wrong, then how can you honestly go forward with full conviction if this is on your conscience? I can't tell you what to do, Richie, but the club has been going downhill for quite some time. We all see it."

I raise my eyes to hers. "As in, the women?"

"Yes, we see and hear everything." She taps her nose. "Pillow talk, baby."

I roll my eyes. "Of course."

"You'd be surprised what I know."

"I sincerely doubt that." I lean up to kiss her. "I don't want to fail you."

Her eyes soften. "You never could."

"But I have, so many times."

"You underestimate me if you think that's even remotely true."

The worst thing for me isn't even dying, it's being locked up for life like Scar and never seeing her or our new baby. I'd miss everything.

There's a tug on my heart to do what's right for the club I love, and to be a man for the family that needs me.

I nod. "I know what I have to do."

"I love you, no matter what." She's always stood by

me. "I'll support your decision." She always knows exactly what to say. "I just want us to be a family, to be happy."

I tilt her chin. "Are we not happy?"

"Yes," she sniffs. "But if the drop has you this worried, then it has me worried too."

I kiss her nose. "You don't have to worry. I'll take care of it."

"Just promise me you'll do what's in your heart, that's all that matters."

"I will. Everything I do is for our future, you and our baby." With all my heart, I mean it.

"When all's said and done, I married you because you're a good man, Richie Hutchison, to the very core. It's your time, baby. You've waited so long for this. I know you don't like friction at the club, but you've always done what's right. That's what makes you different from the rest."

I pull her to my chest as she rolls toward me on her side. "Are you sayin' I'm not a badass?"

She snorts. "You're the most badass man I know, but I also know your heart. I know how much you love the club, but what Skull's doing isn't for the greater good."

Once again, she's right. I didn't marry a dummy.

I kiss her forehead. My heart is racing in my chest. So much is at stake.

There's so much to lose.

I always had my sights on being Prez someday, but I've

been happy being VP, for the most part, especially when Skull started heading down a less sinister and dangerous path with the club. Now, it seems, the club is back to its old ways.

I can't keep looking over my shoulder, wondering when the pigs are gonna come and lock me up, or if I get shot should a drop go bad. How do any of us know how much time we have left? And do I really wanna spend it in a jail cell, or worse, a coffin.

My decision is made.

Kirsty settles into my arms as I hold her.

It's for her.

Everything.

And my unborn baby.

"If you're not with us, then you're against us." Skull isn't happy, but then again, neither am I.

"I don't see it that way." I knew it would come to this. And I came prepared. "I love this club, we're brothers, but I won't see it go down. You know how many of us are in disagreement with the drop, and I've given you my reasons. Aside from the informant who says this deal is shady as fuck, I got a feelin' in my gut. You know my instincts are never wrong."

"If I didn't know any better, it sounds like you want this to go wrong."

I stare at him in disbelief. Out of all the things I thought he was going to say, that wasn't it.

"What are you suggestin'?"

"Both of you, calm down," Harlem says, standing between us. "We can talk about this civilly without anyone gettin' hurt."

Skull moves his focus to Harlem. "Shut the fuck up. The decision is final. We voted. You've made your point, the both of you, and Road King, but this shit ain't gonna stop this drop." He points at me. "You know how good this will be for the club. Man up and do what you're supposed to fuckin' do as my VP and back me up on this, Hutch. I'm not askin'."

I stand my ground. "I won't lead my brothers into a situation I know will be dangerous, not when I know what's at stake."

He reaches around Harlem to try to shove me. "And you think I don't?"

"Not sayin' that, but the drop before this was the last one, and the one before that. You know the pigs are all over this, watchin' us like hawks. We all voted to move this club away from one-percenter business, Skull. Half the club is in jail, or fuckin' dead. What's it gonna take?

"You know what your problem is?" Skull throws at me.

"You let pussy start dictatin', and now she's callin' all the shots because she's carryin' your kid."

"I'll fuckin' kill you!" I lunge at him, managing to shove Harlem enough to get around him.

I punch him hard, once, twice, and as he keeps swinging and missing, my rage knows no bounds.

I keep hitting him until I feel arms around me, pulling me back as Freak holds Skull by the arms.

"Let me fuckin' go!" he yells.

"Take a breath," Freak says, through gritted teeth.

"He just fuckin' hit me! You're a dead man, Hutch, you hear me?"

I stand my ground. More than half this club has my back. Hitting your Prez in any other club would amount to me probably being buried out in the desert, never to be seen or heard from again. But I like to believe the brothers know I do have the club's best interests at heart, I always have. Unlike Skull.

He can say what he wants, but deep down, it's greed deciding for him, not what's best for the club or any of us.

"Just take a beat," Harlem says. "The drop ain't till tomorrow. You'll both have time to cool off. You know Hutch has a point about what he's sayin', Prez, just hear him out. He'd never steer any of us wrong."

Skull glares at Harlem. "Maybe we should take a fuckin' vote right now? See where your loyalties lie."

"Take a beat," Freak agrees. Though I'm sensing he's already planning something. He's got that crazy look in his eyes that I only know too well.

They'll deal with me, I know that much. But for now, I shrug out of Harlem's grip.

I wish the rest of the club were here right now. Not that I want a war, but I want the line I've drawn in the sand to be known. I want the club to pick sides.

I don't fuckin' care anymore. If I'm gonna be partly responsible for something bad happening, then I don't wanna be shy about why.

I know what's gonna happen now. They're gonna try to vote me out.

It won't matter. As much as I love this club, I can't go against my gut.

I never have and I never will. It's the one thing I can rely on, aside from Kirsty.

The one thing that's true.

That's what true brotherhood is.

And I won't break my promise.

Ride or die.

It's now or never.

BRACKEN RIDGE
REBELS
ARIZONA
M · C

CHAPTER 19

HUTCH

The home phone wakes me from my sleep. I crack an eye open, knowing it's late, and I drag myself out of bed to go answer it.

Groggily, I pick up the receiver. "This better be good."

"Shit's gone down, at the quarry," Harlem says down the line.

"What the fuck are you talkin' about?"

"Skull did the drop early."

My head begins to pound. "The fuck?"

I know we didn't leave things on the best of terms between us, but this is low, even for him.

"Moved it up to tonight." By the sound of his voice, this doesn't sound good.

"What are you sayin'?"

"Shootout. I don't know who's dead and who's not. Pigs swarmin'. Better get up here."

"Fuck."

"Looks like Skull's dealer had some overdue debts to

pay with the Mexicans."

"The Mexicans?" I run a hand through my hair.

"This is fucked up. Half the club didn't even know."

"Where are you now?"

"Southeast corner."

"I'll be there in ten minutes."

I hang up, running a hand over my face.

This is the last thing I wanted. Skull, being the greedy fucker he is, changed the plan. We never change the plan. Disagreements aside, we work it out one way or the other.

Dread washes through me.

I didn't want this.

I planned on going along tomorrow, to talk Skull out of it again. We don't need this.

The club is doing fine without getting entangled in a haul too big.

There're other ways to make money. Plenty of ways. What's happened in the last few years is testament enough that we need to move in a different direction. It's what has to happen.

I've had my sights set on the scrapyard for a while. As a club, we can split the costs, and as we build the business up, we split the profits. I've been around long enough to know it can be done.

Kirsty has a couple of shops in her sights that we're thinking about buying as investments too. Completely legit.

There is no other way for this club.

Every time I've tried to talk to Skull about the scrapyard, he shuts me down. It makes me wonder if he was ever interested in going legit or if he was just yanking my, and everyone else's, chain at this club.

I dress quickly as Kirsty turns to look at me in the dark. "Hutch?" she says. "Where are you going?"

I sit on the edge of the bed for a moment, brushing the hair back from her face. "Gotta deal with some club business."

She lets out a deep breath, but doesn't say what she's thinking. I lean down and kiss her. "I love you."

She strokes my face. "I love you too. Hurry home."

I kiss the top of her head and reluctantly leave her side.

Zipping up my cut, I fire up my motorcycle and take off, driving down the deserted street. Anxiety and angst rise within me at the same time. I shake my head.

Stupid fuck.

There was no fuckin' need to do this; the Demons are divided enough as it is. Now there's a goddamn shootout.

I'm a stupid fuck for coming, with the pigs crawling all over the place. Luckily, I know this place better than they do.

The southeast corner is far away enough from the fray to not be seen.

I turn my lights off when I reach the quarry, the cool

night air hitting me full force as I take the gravel road toward where Harlem is waiting. I don't even fuckin' know who is here and who isn't.

I ride for another few minutes before I reach the shrub where I see a row of bikes.

Fuck.

Pulling up, I kick the stand down as I kill the engine.

Harlem greets me as we shoulder bump and, even in the dark, I can see the stress etched across his face.

"How bad is it?"

He shakes his head.

"Skull?"

"Don't know the damage yet."

"What the fuck happened?"

"Road King followed them, called me from the public phone to get the fuck up here, and that's when the shooting started. Seems the intel you had wasn't as far-fetched as we thought."

"Didn't know we were involved with the Mexicans." I palm the back of my head. "This is serious shit." It also makes me wonder, was Skull involved in something else none of us were aware of?

"Seems Skull's been keepin' a lot to himself, and Freak as well, like that comes as a surprise."

As I glance through the trees, I can see cop cars in the distance, lights flashing. This is fucked. It's a helpless feeling. As much as I want to fuckin' strangle Skull right now for doing this, I don't want him dead. I don't want any of my brothers dead.

I'd never put this fuckin' club in danger. I tear at my hair, unsure what the fuck I need to do. I look over and see Road King, Hank, Rainman, Nail and a whole heap of other brothers lined up with them.

Jesus H. Christ.

There's no sign of Spyder, Dog, Grim, Scrooge, or any of the non-committee members.

My brain races.

"They're with you, Hutch." Harlem grasps me on the shoulder. "We all are. What Skull did is crossin' the line that shouldn't have been drawn."

"The committee voted, remember," I remind him. "Over half the club agreed with him. I just don't understand why he moved up the drop."

"Because he wanted more of the profits for himself," Rainman chimes in, coming up beside Harlem. "If we're against him, we don't get shit. Probably thought he could kick us all out and get new members with his pay dirt and all. Seems like he'll be wishin' on a fuckin' star tonight that the pigs didn't pick him. Rather be fuckin' shot than go to prison." He shudders, and my mind reels.

"This is fucked no matter how you look at it."

Harlem asks, "How do you wanna play this?"

I glance around. "Got a prospect handy?"

Harlem shakes his head. "Took those too."

I grimace. Of course he did. They're the most expendable. Probably send them in first, as a human shield.

"We've got no choice," I say after a few moments. "We gotta find out for ourselves."

"You're not seriously sayin' you're gonna go over there while the pigs are swarmin', out lookin' for blood," Rainman says, shaking his head. "It's a bloodbath. No need to be gettin' arrested for not doin' shit."

"Don't plan on gettin' caught," I reply, nodding to Harlem. "We'll move around the outskirts on foot, get a read on what's happenin'. We can't just leave them there."

In the distance, we hear an ambulance, and I close my eyes. I hope to God it ain't for any of our brothers.

I curse Skull for being such a stubborn fuck.

"Agreed," Harlem says. "I'll round up a couple of brothers. We should keep Hank and Rainman here to keep watch, in case the pigs come this way."

I look over to Hank. "Cover up our sleds, just in case.'

"Got it," he says.

"You all right?" Harlem asks, watching me closely as I pinch the bridge of my nose.

Frankly, I'm afraid of what we're gonna find.

"I'll be better when we find out what happened…"

"Let's get goin'," he says.

I never thought I'd dread such simple words, but every part of me is on edge. My blood runs cold when I think about what happened here tonight and why I'll never let greed and ego take over me.

I just hope that some of our brothers got away.

In my heart, I think we all know the outcome.

I stare at Spyder's lifeless body and, even though I didn't like the guy, it's still kinda shocking.

"This is fucked," Harlem whispers as we watch the mayhem unfold around the quarry.

There are bodies everywhere.

Gunfire sure as fuck rained down like fury. I want to know how things went so horribly wrong.

So far, it seems there've been several arrests, but there's still no sign of Skull.

I can't help but think the worst.

"We need to head back to the club," I say to Harlem. "Pronto. We know the protocol."

There's no way we can get any closer without getting snatched ourselves.

We keep low, making the long and tiring route back toward the southeast corner. Somehow, we make it back alive.

"Need to get the fuck outta here," Hank says.

"Just went to check and the pigs will be settin' up roadblocks. We gotta go now," he says, and I know he's right.

We waste no time jumping on our sleds and making our way down the ridge.

The whole way back to the club, taking the tourist drive to avoid more cops, my mind is spinning.

Not surprisingly, when we get there, the club is buzzing with members. The prospect on the gate lets us in, and I know for a fact it won't be long until the cops roll up here, too.

"Not a good fuckin' idea to be here," I mutter to Harlem as he nods.

"Gotta clear out. Pigs will be all over it once they've dealt with the carnage."

When we get inside, I don't see anyone from the committee. My stomach drops.

Then, I see one of the prospects, Weasel, crouched over, blood everywhere.

"What the fuck happened?" I march over, as everyone hovers over him, trying to keep him from squirming around. It don't look fuckin' good.

"Mexicans jumped us," he grits. "Everyone scattered. They took the coke. Fuckers had machine guns…Spyder was right next to me…" Yeah, and we know how that turned out.

"Where's Skull?" I ask, crouching down. We need to get

him to the goddamn emergency room. "Did he make it out?"

He shrugs. "Don't know, it all happened so fast. One minute Skull was checkin' out the goods. The next, a tribe of vans appeared and started shootin' at us."

He looks pale, holding on to his gut as his eyes dart around.

"Need to get you to the hospital," I say. Fuck knows how that's gonna happen without getting him in the shit, too.

"No doctors," he says. "Spiff is gonna get the bullet out."

My eyes go wide. "You can't perform a fuckin' surgery," I bark as Spiff, who knows a little about mechanics but not much else, comes into view.

"What other choice do we have?" he retorts. "Kid's gonna die if I don't."

Weasel's eyes go even rounder. "Am I gonna die?"

This is a fuckin' shitshow.

As I turn, the other members gather around.

"What do we do?" one of the brothers, Jinx, asks.

Truth is, I don't fuckin' know, but we can't let him die on the floor of the clubhouse.

I turn and look at Hank.

Helen. She's a nurse. She's also dumb enough to have Hank Steelman's kid. Jayson is almost seven. Helen got knocked up pretty much straight away, putting her career on hold for a little while when the kid was young. She's not a doctor, but she's our best bet. I don't like involving the ol' ladies, but we got no choice.

"Call your ol' lady," I tell him. "We need her."
He stalls for half a second, then takes off for the door.

I look back at Weasel. "Just hang in there, buddy."

Harlem and I share a look, and he runs a hand over his face.

This is fuckin' grim.

Everyone is quiet. I'm just trying to think about what the right call is.

We need word that some of the brothers are all right. But if they were, they'd be here now.

Just as I'm thinking it, Grouch, another member who took Skull's side, comes running in. He's roughed up, but not bleeding.

I don't want to hear this, but I know I have to.

He tries to catch his breath as we wait for him to get the words out.

"For fuck's sake," Harlem barks. "Out with it. Is Skull okay? Where is everyone?"

Grouch rests his hands on his knees as he raises his face to mine.

I know then. That haunted look in his eyes says it all.

This changes everything.

Forever.

"Skull's dead," Grouch finally spits out. "Everyone's gone or locked up."

Our club President is dead. No fuckin' joke.

"Jesus," I mutter, running both hands through my hair as I tug. "What the fuck was he thinkin'?"

Everyone goes quiet while the news settles.

Stupid, dumb fuck!

Everyone's gone or locked up?

I don't wanna think about what this means, but we need to clear out before the pigs get here.

We'll have to take Weasel with us. We've no choice.

"Clearly, he wasn't," Road King puts in, sitting down on the couch where Weasel lays. "This whole thing just fuckin' blows."

Skull is…dead?

I let the words sink in, knowing nothing I can say will bring any of the brothers back, that none of it can be undone.

This club is in more disarray than I thought.

"We need to move out," I say, getting my shit together. We've got time to wonder and speculate later. "Now!"

Everyone jumps up, aside from poor Weasel. It doesn't look good for him, but I don't have the heart to say shit.

"It's gonna be okay," I tell him, knowing that it's all lies. "I promise."

The last words he hears should be something he can hold on to.

It's a lie I want to believe it myself. To make it all go away. To make things the way they were.

But I can't. Those days are gone.

Nothing is ever gonna be the same again.

CHAPTER 20

KIRSTY

THREE MONTHS LATER

They place our baby in my arms, and I stare down at her in wonder.

Hutch cradles her hand with his hand, cupping her tiny head. I can't believe how small she is, though she didn't feel small coming out of me.

I had a long labor, but I'm so relieved she was delivered without complication. I don't think I've ever been so exhausted in my life. And Hutch was beside me the entire time. I thought he was going to faint when she was actually born.

"A baby girl," Hutch whispers, kissing her head.

"Hey, that's my pet name." I laugh as his eyes meet mine.

"She's perfect, Kirst."

She really is.

She has a flock of light hair, just like her daddy. Her nose is like mine, and she has both our blue eyes.

"She looks smart," I agree.

"She looks like her mama, thank Christ. Except for

the hair."

His lips brush mine as I hold her.

"Did we do this?" I chuckle.

"Oh, baby, we did it. I remember all the practice we had."

He sits on the edge of the bed, one arm around me and his hand still cradling our little girl.

"I'm so happy," I say, tears filling my eyes.

"Me too, she's our little miracle."

Seeing Hutch as a dad, I don't think anything could be more satisfying.

He needed this.

A change of pace.

After everything went down with the club recently, I'm surprised he's still on his feet.

Skull, and half the Demons, died in the shootout. Several other members were held in custody, awaiting trial. It was a mess of epic proportions.

The cops raided the club, but they didn't find anything to pin the other members with. The clubhouse was clean. Even the prospect, Weasel, who ended up dying on the way to see Helen with his gunshot wounds, was disposed of without a trace.

I don't honestly want to know. But the time for change couldn't come soon enough.

I thank my lucky stars that Hutch didn't go through with the deal and stood his ground. I don't know where we'd be right now, but it's not somewhere good.

I'm just glad it's over.

I'm sad Hutch's brothers died, I really am. But a lot of them were very bad men. Men I didn't like. Men I didn't want to be left alone in a room with. And to me, a club shouldn't feel like that. It's always been Richie's dream to be a family, a real brotherhood with the club. Being able to trust your brothers is something that's paramount, something he craves more than anything.

I support him fully.

And that's why the remaining members of the committee made him the new president. They discarded the Demons and they've started a new club, filtering out those that didn't fit with the new club rules.

The Bracken Ridge Rebels.

Hutch is friends with a few of the other legit clubs in the various chapters around the country, and they were only too happy to have Bracken Ridge join forces. They welcomed it with open arms.

I know the loss of his brothers has weighed heavily on his mind. He hasn't been himself since the night he left after getting the phone call.

He wonders if he did the right thing. The fight he had with Skull right before he took matters into his own hands. The way the divide split them in the end.

I know he's always wanted the club to be legit, but

I also know he didn't want this. Skull went back on everything he promised, choosing more money over doing what was right. He never wanted the club to be legit like Hutch thought. It was all a ruse to become Prez after Scar was locked up.

It's only been a short time, but the brothers are slowly gaining traction. For one, cleaning up the clubhouse, with a lot of help from the ol' ladies and some of the sweet butts.

It was long overdue.

Hutch wants to put money back into the club, fix things, make the clubhouse something to be proud of for the existing and new members. The land is owned by Max Morgan, he's a slimeball who refuses to sell, but at least he lets the clubhouse sit there for cheap rent.

I'm so proud of Hutch.

When he got voted in, he wasn't sure if he even wanted it anymore. There was so much loss in the club, so much turbulence. He'd turned to me and said, "I don't know how to do anything else, Kirst, this club is my blood. It's my life. What am I without them?"

Of course, I reassured him that he was enough without the club, but being from a broken home, I knew he craved the family aspect. He wanted his family back.

I glance up and Hutch is staring at me.

"You okay, daddy?"

He smirks. "Better not call me that, I think I might like

it a little too much."

I roll my lips. "Did I tell you I love you today?"

"Not yet." He leans over. "Give daddy a little sugar."

We kiss lightly and then the baby lets out a scream that makes us both jump.

Hutch looks down. "She's got lungs on her like her mama, too."

I've no idea what to do with a baby, but the nurse comes over, and Hutch let's her fuss while she helps me give the baby her first feed.

Hutch stares at us in wonder, his face full of so much love I want to burst.

Hutch, of course, has been loving my body while pregnant. The rounder, the better; the man has barely been able to keep his hands off me. And I love it, the same way I always have and always will.

He's my man. And I'm his woman.

"Deanna," Hutch says. "She looks like Deanna."

I glance down at her, her beautiful little button nose and soft pink skin.

Deanna was one of our top five names. And I have to say, it really does suit her.

"I love it," I say, beaming at him.

"Can't wait to get you home," he murmurs close to my ear, so the nurse can't hear.

Even like this, he's as badass as they come. And I love

him, with all my heart, I love him.

"Me either," I muse, fussing with my daughter's hair.

She really is perfect.

Our little miracle.

Nothing else from here on out matters. Just that we stick together. We keep moving forward. We keep our hearts together, striving to be better people. To love more.

That's all I've ever wanted.

And finally, I have it.

Watching my husband and Deanna together is like a dream come true.

He's completely hands-on. Holding her, soothing her when she cries, putting her to bed, feeding her with a bottle, even changing her diaper. It is the cutest, sweetest thing I've ever seen.

Daddy Hutch.

It's like he was born to do this.

I had no idea he was going to be this hands on, and it warms my heart, especially when I hear them together when he thinks I'm not there. He sings to her. Plays with her, reads her books. He tickles her and tries to make her giggle. And he's very, very protective, as I knew he would be. But I think he's way worse now than he ever was before. Gotta love me a daddy alpha male. It suits him.

I'd love to give him a dozen more kids if this is what it brings out in him.

I can imagine a whole tribe of kids at our feet, and Hutch's leg being tugged on while everyone vies for his attention.

I love what a natural he is.

He looks up, his finger in her mouth as she sucks on it.

"What?"

I shake my head.

"What?" He grins.

"Can't a woman just enjoy her husband being Daddy of the Year?"

He scoffs. "I don't think I'm that."

"She loves you."

She really does. She always stops crying when he picks her up, not so much for me.

Daddy's little girl.

A grin spreads across my face.

"I hope so. I hope I'm not gonna ever disappoint her."

I shake my head. "Not possible."

"Kids make you wanna be better," he says, looking down at her as she looks up at him.

"I know."

"I want to give her everything."

"We already have everything, with you here, our

protector."

He nods. I know how strongly he feels about this.

It's his role.

Even more so than being Prez in the MC. He was born to protect his family.

"I'll never let anythin' happen to the two of you," he states firmly. "You've given me everything, Kirst. Everything I could ever want."

I bask in the afterglow. A new baby in the house, everything fresh at the club, it feels like a rebirth in a lot of ways.

And Hutch seems happier. Even if he has been taking things a little easier at the club since Deanna and I came home.

He wants to be there, every step of the way.

I never want things to change.

Not ever.

This is our piece of paradise, and I'm going to swim in it.

I feel so lucky.

Life isn't perfect, but then again, what is?

My parents didn't even come and see the new baby. I'm at least hoping my dad will look in, even if my mother won't. She has never agreed with our union and has never been supportive. Not even with her first grandkid coming into the world.

That part saddens me. That she'll never know

grandparents or have that whole experience. But I would never keep her from them. I want them to be part of her life. I just won't let my mom anywhere near her without being there. The last thing I want is my baby growing up thinking she's less than because she doesn't fit my mother's mold. I know my mom did her best; I guess she only knows what she knows from her own upbringing. But that's no excuse. Love is love.

Maybe in time, it will change. I can only hope. The door is always open.

For now, it's all about us. And that's the only thing that matters.

FIVE YEARS LATER

"Helen, you're going to have to go in there," I say. She's heavily pregnant, but I know if I go inside that house, where Joshua and Amanda are, I will fold.

The kids aren't directly associated with the club, but they go to the same school as Deanna. And somebody has to step in when child welfare won't.

We've just had the worst possible news about what's been going on, and aside from being mistreated and their crack-whore of a mom not stopping their abuse, we've learned they're also being molested.

My gut clenches as I fight back tears. I wasn't made for this. I swear to God.

I just can't even imagine that kind of environment and how bad it's been for them.

"It's okay, I'll go in," Helen says. "I know them. Joshua will take a little bit of coaxing, but he'll come out. He'll be safe now."

I nod, feeling like a failure.

The sliding door opens, and Hutch stands there, his eyes finding mine.

Seeing my distress, he tilts my chin with his hand. "You okay, baby girl?"

I shake my head. "I'm sorry. I'm just not strong enough."

He nods. "I'll bring Amanda first."

I begin to shake. This is a hard limit for me, and I feel like a failure because this isn't about me. It's about those two innocent kids.

Hutch pulls me into a one-armed hug.

"It's gonna be put right, Kirst," Cash says, as I fold into my husband's arms.

Cash is a good man. Hutch and he first met when Cash was prospecting at another club and their paths collided. They've been good friends ever since.

He's just started his own club down in New Orleans. But Hutch needed back-up for a job like this.

A job that requires taking out the trash.

"Don't cry. We'll have them soon, okay?" Hutch kisses the top of my head.

"Ready?" Brock asks, the new prospect for the club. He's thick, burly, and Hutch's shadow.

The club has come so far in the last five years. New members coming and older members leaving. But the Bracken Ridge Rebels are thriving. Hutch has been the touchstone this club needed, and I'm so proud of him.

Hutch turns over his shoulder. "Ready."

"Be safe," I whisper.

He kisses me chastely. "I'll be right back."

Helen steps out, patting me on the arm, and they disappear into the rundown house to rescue two kids who should have never been put in this position to begin with.

Not for the first time, I ask myself how the world can be so cruel.

But I never get an answer.

BRACKEN RIDGE
REBELS
ARIZONA
M · C

CHAPTER 21

HUTCH

I've had to do some pretty shitty things in my lifetime thus far, but this is something I'm actually proud of.

Ending this piece of shit for what he's done is exactly what I stand for. I don't believe there is redemption for people who hurt kids…who…no, don't fuckin' go there.

I want him to suffer, as Amanda and Joshua have, and suffer he will.

I circle him, tied to a chair in the backyard.

The kids are out in the car. Kirsty and Helen are taking them to get burgers, as the poor kids haven't probably eaten in a week. Deanna is with Ginger, one of the chicks who works at the bar, and her old man Grizz, they're like the grandparents Deanna never had. God bless them. I didn't wanna have to involve Helen, being Hank skipped out on her, leaving her pregnant and Jayson being a wayward teenager, but it was her who first noticed bruises and marks on them at the hospital.

To think that someone could do this to a child is

beyond anything I could ever imagine. This is gonna be slow and painful.

I stare at Brock. He's only seventeen, and he's never killed before, but this kid is built like his old man and could be a linebacker for the 49ers. Now it's time to make him a man.

Cash lays punches into his ribs, then his nose, then Brock takes over as they tag team.

The beating is brutal, as this piece of shit whose name is irrelevant, squirms in the chair, his hands tied behind his back, a gag in his mouth.

I can't inflict enough pain, though I wish I could, but if I do he'll die too quickly.

"You think you can hurt kids?" Cash roars in his face, spitting on his boots. "You sick fuck!"

Brock stops his ministrations, and I know it's because the dude is about to pass out. Nobody wants that. We need him conscious.

Brock turns to me. I see the pain in his eyes. He knows little Joshua from being around the club sometimes. He and Jayson shoot hoops. He's a good kid. A nice kid. Sunshine, I always called him. Not like his little sister, who's always shy and won't speak to anybody. Poor little Amanda. My heart breaks all over again picturing her little face when I carried her out of that room and gave her to Helen. Joshua took a little bit of coaxing, he's a good kid, hiding his sister in the closet. Breathe, or you'll never get this over with.

Anger boils in my blood as I think of how many days and nights they've had to suffer.

I turn away, taking a moment to compose myself.

Neither Brock nor Cash say a word.

This is between me and God, and I sometimes wonder how he could let anything like this ever happen. To a child? This is fucked on so many levels. I question a lot of things when it comes to the human race but this is beyond comprehension.

When I picture little Amanda, hiding in the cupboard where Joshua had hidden her, thinking it was that bastard again, it brings tears to my eyes. And the first and only few times I ever cried was when I married Kirsty and when Deanna was born.

I crack my neck.

"You okay, H?" Cash asks. I feel his hand on my shoulder.

I clear my throat. "I'm good."

"Let's finish this. We'll take his body to the quarry. I'll show Brock how to do it properly. You go check on the kids and the women."

I nod.

Cash is my best friend. He's a few years younger than me, but we've always gotten along. We don't see each other much these days, but when we do, it's like no time has passed at all.

I wanted him here. I wanted this to be just us. He is one of the only people I trust in this world with my club, my wife and my daughter.

I owe it to those kids.

And that fuckin' deadbeat woman they call a mama.

She should be fuckin' shot too.

"Prez?" Brock says. Our eyes meet.

"You ever kneecapped a man, son?"

Brock shakes his head. To his credit, he doesn't look afraid. If anything, he looks like he might enjoy it.

Fuckface starts to squirm again.

"Move one more time, and I'll cut your dick off," I bark. I can't take much more of this. I thought I wanted this to drag on, like how it's dragged on for Joshua and Amanda, but now I just want him off the face of the earth. I don't want him breathing the same air as any one of us.

"There's a special place in hell for people like you," Cash says, circling him, taunting him. "But before you get there, we're gonna inflict a little more pain on you ourselves. Call it a parting gift. You like to hurt little kids? Well, we like to hurt people like you, just to remind you that good will always win over evil, fuckface."

Cash snaps his arm so far out of his shoulder, I wince.

He howls in pain behind his gag.

I nod to Brock. He's been learning how to shoot. Taking

the gun out from behind the back of his jeans, he lines it up, just like I taught him. He fires, the bullet making a god-awful sound as fuckface howls, withering around like he's a dying man. Oh, death will come to him soon.

Cash is in his ear again. "That feel good, buddy? Next one goes into your dick."

He screams, or tries to, but nobody hears. Nobody out here is gonna hear shit.

Brock stares at him indifferently, like none of this affects him. He's gonna make a mighty fine VP one day soon. He's someone I can trust, someone who, even though he's still young, has proven time and time again, he's loyal and reliable. This is exactly what this club needs.

Someone who will take action and do the things that need to be done.

I can't stop the images. I just can't.

I take the gun off Brock and aim it at his crotch. I fire. Blood spurts everywhere, covering me, my boots. But I don't stop even when his screams pierce the night air. I fire at his chest. Once. Twice. Three times.

Then his head. Over and over, until he slumps, and even then…I fire until there are no more bullets left.

Until my eyes meet Cash's, and he gives me a chin lift. "It's over, Hutch."

I swallow hard, my eyes closing for a moment.

Adrenaline courses through me as I stare at the asshole

slumped in the chair.

It isn't even justice, nothing is.

"Make sure he's never found," I say. Cash nods, his eyes meeting Brock's. "And make sure all this blood is cleaned up, Brock. Less of a mess we make, the better, not that the cops won't be secretly thankin' me for this one."

"Got it, Hutch." Even I can hear the regret in his tone that this didn't drag out longer.

I couldn't. I have to get back to those kids, and my own. They need me.

I turn and walk away, taking the gun with me.

Deanna crawls into my lap.

"Did you have a nice time at Ginger and Grizz's?" I kiss her nose as she wraps her arms around my neck.

"Yes! And Uncle Grizz gave me Cheetos for dinner."

I give her a look as she giggles. I start to tickle her, knowing she's trying her best to get the old man in trouble, not that it would take much.

"Joshua and Amanda will be stayin' for a little while with us, all right, baby?"

"Okay, Daddy."

"So you have to let Amanda and Joshua play with your toys if they want to. Remember how mama said we have to be kind and share? Amanda is very shy, so you've got to be her very special friend and help her, okay?"

She nods.

"That would make Daddy very proud."

"Can we have Cheetos?"

I shake my head. This kid. Then I concede, "Maybe."

"For breakfast?" She starts to dance around in my lap. Keeping this kid still is impossible. She wears a tutu with leggings underneath and huge butterfly wings, matched with her favorite snow boots.

She's the ultimate princess meets tomboy.

"Just don't tell Mommy." I give her a wink.

She falls into my arms as I rock her. Sometimes she does this. She just wants to be cradled, and when we're like this, me and my daughter, there's no greater feeling in the world. I hope she'll always be at the stage where she wants my attention, though I know as she grows older, I'll become someone she will probably want to yell and scream at. Especially when she learns she won't be datin' until she's forty…or when I'm dead.

"Daddy?"

"Yes, princess."

"Will you color with me?"

We just got her a new paint set, and she's mad about it. She loves to paint and make crazy collages, sticking things to the piece of paper that she gives to people to decorate their fridges. I swear one day this kid is going to be the next Michelangelo.

"Of course I will." I gave her a smile, and she gives me a big kiss in return. "Are you Daddy's girl?"

She giggles in reply.

I tickle her again. I try not to think about how some kids aren't loved like this, how some kids have it fuckin' rough, and I can't. I don't ever wanna think about that day ever again.

Joshua and Amanda will be in our care for the moment, until we can work out what the fuck is gonna happen. One thing is for sure, they're not going into foster care.

Not a fuckin' chance.

These kids deserve a little normalcy for a while. The chance to just be kids. Go to sleep at night in a warm bed without the fear of anyone hurting them. It's a basic human right…I stare at my daughter as she climbs off my knee and wanders over to her dollhouse.

"Here, Daddy," she says, handing me a plastic teacup, which she pretends to fill up from the matching teapot. "Cuppy coffee."

"Thank you, darlin'," I say, taking the tiny cup and pretending to sip it. "Mmm, best cuppy I ever had."

"Daddy!" she screeches as I stop pretending to be sipping. "I forgot the sugar!"

I roll my eyes. "Oops."

I hold my cup out as she grabs the giant wooden spoon she's taken from the kitchen and proceeds to load my tiny cup with spoonfuls of pretend sugar.

"There you go!"

I take another sip. "Ahh, that's better."

The front door opens and closes, and then I hear voices. Kirsty and the kids.

I turn back to Deanna. "Best behavior," I tell her sternly. "Make Daddy proud."

She nods earnestly. "Okay, Daddy."

I stand as Kirsty comes in. Joshua holds her hand while she has Amanda cradled around her. She's like a koala, not letting go, her face buried in my wife's shoulder. I don't blame her for being afraid of men.

A tightness in my chest makes it hard to breathe as I take them in.

Joshua gives me a small smile.

"Hey!' Deanna cries, suddenly busying herself at the dollhouse. "Do you wanna play with my toys?"

Joshua watches what she's doing. He's only seven, and Amanda's five, the same age as Deanna. My heart lurches… the same age as Deanna.

"What is that?" Joshua asks, as Deanna hands him a cup.

"It's a tea set, silly."

"Deanna," I warn.

She slaps a hand over her mouth, but Joshua laughs.

He's a good kid. Smart for his age. He indulges her, walking over as she hands him a cup and a Barbie.

I turn to my wife. "Is she asleep?"

Kirsty nods. I move over to her, leaving the kids to play. "There's some paperwork to fill in, but we'll get there."

We don't speak about the hospital visit. None of us need to revisit that and the trauma these kids have gone through.

I cup my wife's face. "I'll love you forever, Kirsty Hutchinson."

"Not as much as I love you, Richie."

I smile. "I've set the bunks up in the spare room."

"Thank you."

I turn to watch Deanna and Joshua, a smile forming as they have their own little tea party.

"Think they'll be okay?"

Kirsty kisses Amanda on the head. "They will be now."

I nod, knowing it's true.

I want to adopt them, but being Prez of a motorcycle club and having a criminal record, even if they are petty charges, I doubt that's ever gonna happen. I don't wanna think about that right now, though.

All that matters is they're here, they're safe, and nothing else bad is gonna happen.

Over my dead body.

I put an arm around Kirsty's shoulders. "You're right, baby girl. I just wanna make sure they know it's safe."

"They will," she whispers. "It's just gonna take time, that's all."

I swallow the lump in my throat. My protective stance is in full flight.

If anyone looks sideways at these kids, I'll fuckin' kill them. Just like I did that asshole.

And that's a promise I'll take to the grave.

BRACKEN RIDGE
REBELS
ARIZONA
M · C

CHAPTER 22

Looking out of my office window that faces the main street of town, I watch people passing by, going about their days.

I check the time, dreading that it's almost two o'clock. Then I hear straight pipes, and my anxiety waivers just a little bit.

Hutch always makes me feel calm.

The years have been good to us. We split for a year when Deanna was growing up; not a time I care to remember fondly, but pressures of the club made living with him at times impossible. He's dove headfirst into the club, after making sure Summer and Gunner, who they're now named, were looked after. I know all of what happened took its toll. I think he had PTSD, but didn't seek help.

His drinking got worse. He couldn't handle what he saw that day with those kids.

And like a coward, I had to walk away. I never thought

we'd ever be in a position to split up. In hindsight, it only brought us closer together, but it was like torture for those months away from one another.

I thought our love could withstand anything, but one thing I know about life is it tests you.

I never gave up on us, and neither did Hutch.

Deanna getting sick when she was small turned everything around, and we've never been stronger.

And then there's Jake, or Gears, as he goes by.

Hutch's kid.

I love him, and I don't hold anything against him, or Hutch, even though he's not my own child.

Hutch fell into the arms of another woman while we were separated on a drunken night at the club. A night he doesn't even remember. It only happened once, and he never knew about Gears until just recently. She hid it from him, never wanting anything in return, and then she passed away when he was small. He never got to know about Gears until it happened by chance. Gears had been prospecting for the club for almost a year when it all came about.

I always knew about the indiscretion, he told me straight away once we were back together, and I didn't blame him. We'd been apart for almost a year. I left him. Sure, I was hurt. I may have even punished him in a way, but deep down, I knew he was lost. We both were. The years had caught up with us, and I should have tried to stick things out, instead of leaving. He'd tried many times to get me to come back, but I needed to see a real change in him. He wanted so much for the club to be something, it's his legacy, and somewhere in the mix, everything became hazy. When Deanna was sick, everything shifted.

He still is a good man.

I'll never forget when he was on his hands and knees, begging me to come back. He quit drinking. Quit spending so much time at the club, learning how to be a family again, but he could never separate the two for many years. He told me everything. Even the parts that he didn't want me to know. I've never seen him in such a state.

We dug deep. Both of us. Remembering how we used to be when we were first together. How much he adored me and I him, and we started again. We built our family back together.

I know he was traumatized, that one incident with the kids altered him in so many ways, but Summer and Gunner grew up never knowing anything but love from then on. They were adopted by a wonderful lady named Gloria, who now lives down in Florida. In time, they healed and became fantastic kids.

Now that Gunner and Summer are both grown, we've both enjoyed seeing them turn into fine young adults. Summer actually did a lot better than Gunner as she came out of her shell. He took a lot longer than we expected to learn to trust, and he still has anger issues toward his birth mom. She ended up overdosing not long after, not that it was any great loss after what she let happen to them.

Deanna is twenty-six now and runs her own small business interior decorating and designing. We're both so proud of her and she's the apple of her daddy's eye, she always was. We just both wish she'd settle down soon. I can't wait to have some grandkids running around.

The straight pipes get closer, and thrill runs through me. The same way it always does when he's here to collect me.

I may be fifty-four, but I still have the love of a good man behind me. A man I've only grown to love more and more.

The sound suddenly disappears, and I know he's parking. A few moments later, I see him pass my window.

Hutch.

He's still the man of my dreams.

Dressed in his cut with a black Henley, leather pants, black boots, and a bandana around his long hair, he's still the only man I could ever want, the one who turns my eye.

He only got sexier as the years went by.

He still rocks it.

Even though he's a lot grayer these days, he still has the power to bring me to my knees.

The front door chimes, and he takes up all the room in the doorjamb of my office.

I turn my face to greet him. "Hi, baby."

He smiles, his face is soft, full of concern…he knows what today means too. We both do.

"Hi, baby girl. You got some sugar for me?"

I can't help but smile as he approaches, sitting his fine ass on my desk. He leans down, and I lean up, meeting him halfway. We kiss, softly, tentatively. I know he's afraid he'll break me, and I don't like it.

"You don't have to do that," I say when we break away.

"Do what?" He frowns.

"Kiss me like I'm fragile."

He swallows hard. "We don't wanna be late."

I nod. "Okay."

He watches me, concern etched on his face.

I know he's worried about me, but I feel strong.

Today we have to go to the doctor and get my diagnosis.

Breast cancer, or so they think.

I try not to show how shit scared I am. We haven't even told Deanna, not until we know for sure. Hutch and I never had more kids, not because we didn't want them, but I wasn't able to carry after my complicated pregnancy with Deanna. So now I'm mother hen to everyone in the club, and their kids instead. And Gears and I get along great. He's exactly like his father.

And we are a real family.

Our daughter, Deanna, who continues to live a single

and carefree life, much to her father's dismay, makes us proud living her dreams.

Our son Gears, who fell in love with Amelia, Brock and Axton's little sister.

Summer, who's now training to be a nurse and moving to New Orleans.

Gunner married Steel's sister, Lily.

Steel and Sienna, and their fur babies.

Brock and Angel and their kids, Rawlings, Ethan Wolf, and Amber Jane.

Rubble and Lucy and their kid, Avery, and she's pregnant again.

Axton and Stevie, who's heavily pregnant.

Bones and Kennedy, who are trying for a baby.

Colt and Cassidy, and their fur baby.

Nitro and Frankie, who's also pregnant, and their daughter, Raven.

Grizz and Ginger are still around, as well as Dalton and Patch, who are long-time members. Harlem went to join Cash in New Orleans, and other club members dropped off over the years or retired. But here we all are.

Still breathing.

Still a family.

"You okay, Kirst?"

I smile, cupping his face as I grab my purse. "Yes, of course."

He swallows roughly, and I know it's hard for him to see me like this. Not knowing what's going to happen and ultimately me being sick.

He pulls me to him. "No matter what happens, baby, I love you. Do you hear me?"

I kiss him softly. "Not as much as I love you."

He smiles, but it doesn't reach his eyes. "This isn't how it was supposed to be as we near retirement," he mumbles, our foreheads touching. "We don't even have grandkids yet."

I laugh. "Blame your wayward daughter for that. I think we will have better luck with Amelia and Gears."

He sighs. "I just want one grandkid."

"You have several at the club."

"That's true, but I think kids would ground her."

"No, I think the right man should come first."

It's like he's forgotten how this works.

He screws up his face. "I don't want to think about it."

Deanna will always be his little girl, no matter what. I pity the poor man who comes along. He won't know what hit him.

They're very close. She adores him and always has. He's the only one she pretends to listen to. She's had me on the bench for years, but she lets her daddy win a couple of rounds. Just to make him think he still has some control over her life, when really, he has none.

She's a good kid, but we both know she can be wild. She likes to cover up her fear of being loved by anyone by finding Mr. Right Now, instead of Mr. Right. If her dad knew half of what I know…

Hutch stands, holding out his hand. "We need to go, don't wanna be late."

I sigh, taking his hand as he leads me out. "I'll see you tomorrow," I say to Kelsey, who's manning the desk this afternoon. Kelsey is the teenager who babysits Brock and Angel's kids, as well as helps out around all of our businesses. She's the daughter of one of my good friends.

"Bye, Kirsty. See ya, Hutch."

Hutch gives her the peace sign as I wave.

We get to Hutch's motorcycle, and he hands me my helmet, helping it onto my head. Once again…not needed, but I let him. Ever since we had this scare, he's been overly protective. That's the only way he knows how to be.

It's how he shows he cares. And I love him for it.

He fastens it for me before securing his own, then swings his leg over, kicks up the stand, and starts the beast. And what a sound it is.

Even the cops don't bother to stop him anymore. They know us by now.

Hutch is even good friends with Chief Jenkins.

I climb on behind him. I never pass up the opportunity to ride with him. When I'm on the back of his bike, it's like

I'm eighteen again and have nothing but wild abandon and the open road between us.

I will never get sick of this.

He drives carefully to the doctor's office. I refused to see a doc in Phoenix, even though Hutch wanted me to. I like my doctors here; they're perfectly capable.

When we arrive, he takes my hand as we sit in the waiting room.

It feels like an eternity until Doctor Jenny Greaves calls us in. We're on a first name basis, being good friends.

We sit at her desk while she stacks the papers in front of her. Hutch holds my hand, resting it on his knee. "I'm afraid it's as we feared," she says as my heart plummets into my stomach.

Hutch goes rigid.

I try to contain my emotions.

"You have stage one breast cancer, Kirsty." She pauses as I stare at her. "But the thing to remember is that we've caught it early, and at this stage, no cancer cells have been found in the lymph nodes, or other parts of the body."

"At this stage?" Hutch cuts in. "So, it could happen?"

She looks at him. "It's early stages, Hutch. We caught it early, this is good. It means we can treat it."

He stands, unable to sit any longer, running a hand through his hair.

I stare up at him.

"What needs to happen?" he barks at her.

"Hutch," I say calmly. "Please."

He turns to look at me, and I know he's gonna lose it. I just hope Jenny's desk isn't the recipient of his anger.

"I'm sorry, baby girl, I just wanna know if you're gonna be okay…I can't…" he trails off.

I hold out my hand, and he takes a second before he moves toward me, grabbing my hand and pressing a kiss to it as he sits back down.

Jenny has known us both long enough to understand who he is, so his reaction is no shock to her.

"I know," I say to him in a soft voice. "But like Jenny said, we've caught it early. We can treat it. It doesn't mean…"

He glances at me. He won't let me say it.

He doesn't exist in a world I'm not in.

Our love is too strong.

We mean too much to each other.

Through thick and thin, we're still here. Forever.

"It doesn't mean the worst," I continue.

"Kirsty's right, we're going to go through all the treatment plans, including surgery, radiotherapy, chemotherapy and hormonal therapy. We can discuss all the options at length, and I can answer any questions you may have."

Hutch swallows hard.

"He wants to know what the survival rate is," I choke out.

Hutch glances at me sharply.

I said it. He won't, but we both wanna know. We can't be google doctors forever, and I know Hutch has thrown himself into researching everything, insisting we make fresh juices every morning, take vitamin C shots, and even going on a vegan diet.

I cannot imagine my mountain man eating a cauliflower steak with a side order of mung beans. Somehow, I know that's not gonna happen, but bless his heart for trying anything to get me well again.

"The most important thing is we stay positive about the diagnosis," she says, looking from me to Hutch. "Like I said, we've caught it early and have a whole range of treatments we can explore. The survival rate is very high for stage one breast cancer. We will need to start a treatment plan soon, so you have time to consider your options."

How are we going to tell Deanna?

Dread fills me. She'll be devastated.

As if reading my mind, Hutch squeezes my hand, linking his fingers through mine. Now is the time I need my man to be strong. I'm not ashamed to say that I need him to lean on, so we can both get through this together.

I look at him as he gives me that same look he used to, back when we were just a couple of kids who had no idea what the future would bring.

We can get through this. We have to.

BRACKEN RIDGE
REBELS
ARIZONA
M · C

CHAPTER 23

HUTCH

PRESENT DAY

Deanna folds into her mother's arms as I look away. Not many things choke me up, but looking at my girls in a moment of what feels like despair is just too much.

I step outside.

The cool air hits me in the face like an old friend. I grasp the front railing of the porch, the pounding in my ears feeling like my head may combust.

Why does the fuckin' world gotta be so cruel?

Gears follows me.

"You okay, Pops?"

I wipe my eyes, then turn to face him. He grips my shoulder, concern written all over his face.

He loves Kirsty. She's been like a mother to him ever since we found out the one mistake I ever made in life resulted in his conception.

When Kirsty and I separated, I got close to his mom, we

were friends. She was a good woman, cleaned at the club, didn't sleep around, looked after me in a motherly kinda way. One night, we'd had too much to drink and, truth be told, I didn't even remember what fuckin' happened until the next morning when we woke up. It was the first and only time I've ever slept with a woman other than my wife since I got together with Kirsty. I felt so horribly guilty. So did she. We parted as friends, and she left Bracken Ridge shortly after. She never told me she was pregnant, and I'll never understand why.

When Deanna got sick shortly after, it was a wakeup call to change my ways. Stop drinking and get my family back, and that's what I did. I made changes to get myself on a better track.

I quit drinking so hard. I quit a lot of bad shit.

I couldn't use Summer and Gunner's trauma as an excuse, even though I know I took everything that happened to them to heart. For years, it wrecked me. I couldn't understand how anyone could do that, and I spiraled. Forgetting about the ones who needed me most.

I told Kirsty that I'd slept with another woman, and for some unknown reason, she forgave me. It didn't matter to me that we were separated, and it had been almost a year without her in my bed, it should never have happened. I take full responsibility. There has only ever been her. Kirsty is the one woman I respect and look up to. We're strong.

Except right now, I feel lost. Like I want to make this all better, but I can't.

It's wrecking me.

"I've been better, Son."

He's a lot like me, my kid. He's good. Handsome as fuck and he's got a kind heart. His mama did a good job; I just wish she'd have told me about him. That part I'll never truly get over, especially when I think about all I missed out on not seeing him grow up.

He squeezes my shoulder. "Wanna talk about it?"

I shrug. "What is there to say? Won't make it any better."

"Sometimes it helps to get shit off your chest."

I give him a look. "Since when did you get so philosophical?"

"I get my brains from my mom."

I pull him into my chest and get him in a headlock, scruffing his hair like he's five years old. "Have some respect for your old man."

He struggles, laughing as I let him go. "Pops, don't mess with the hair."

I put my arm around his shoulders as we stand and stare at the backyard.

"When you gonna give me some grandkids?"

He rolls his eyes. "Deanna's older than me. She should be the one givin' you the first few."

"My daughter is still five years old with pigtails," I tell him. "At least in my mind."

He smirks. "She'll settle one day."

Running a hand through his hair, I shift my gaze back to him. "What's on your mind?"

I know something's up, but it could just be because both my kids just found out about Kirsty's diagnosis.

"Nothin'."

"You think you can lie to me?"

"Just worried."

I know something else is going on.

"Jake."

He blows air out of his cheeks. "Bringin' out the big guns, old man, callin' me by my real name."

"Let's just say, I've been around the block a time or two. I can smell bullshit a mile away."

Then he says something that makes my blood run cold. "Deanna will kill me."

I turn to him. "What's going on?"

"I don't wanna do this here." He thumbs over his shoulder toward the house.

"Fuck's sake, do I have to shake it out of you?"

I'm met with more silence as he deliberates what he has to tell me.

"I think Deanna's being stalked."

My eyes go wide. "What the fuck?"

"She asked me to stay over the last few nights, and I thought it was because she wanted to catch up with Amelia bein' out of town with Kennedy. We had a couple of drinks, and she confessed that she thinks this guy she hooked up with has been following her."

I stare at him, unable to fathom why it took him this long to come and tell me.

"And you found this out?"

"Last night."

"And you didn't come to me?"

"In my defense, my sister didn't want you to know."

"I'm her father. I have every right to know."

"Pops, please don't say anything. You'll just make it worse."

"Do you think it's true?"

"I don't know, but I've never seen D so jumpy."

I rub my chin. "Watch her. I'll put the prospects on her tail for a little bit. Do you know who the guy is?"

"She wouldn't tell me his name, but I'll pry it out of her."

I'm furious. Does Deanna think so little of me that I'd do anything to put her in harm's way? By not telling me, that's exactly what she's doing.

If she weren't in there hugging her mom right now after finding out she's got cancer, I'd haul her ass out here and demand answers.

"Don't let her out of your sight," I tell him.

"She's gonna notice if…"

"I don't give a shit. There's some crazy fuckers around. If she thinks she's unsafe, then chances are, she is. Especially if she asked you to stay over. That's not like her."

She must have been spooked. Deanna is a strong, independent woman. I joke about her being my little girl, but I also know how headstrong she can be. Always wanting to do things for herself and not asking for help when she needs it.

I didn't fuckin' instill that part into her. She can always come to me.

"I know, that's why I did it. We could always get Linc to…" he trails off as I look at him.

"Hack into her phone?"

Gears shrugs. "Maybe."

I pinch the bridge of my nose. Is my daughter too proud to come to me if some weirdo is harassing her? Surely, she would. I don't believe she's getting messages, nor do I believe that we should snoop on her messages, but I store it away for later, just in case.

"She'll have our balls if she finds out."

"Or I could snoop around, when she's at work."

I point at him. "Good idea. I need his name, that's all. Surely, you can do that."

"Maybe I can get her phone, check the hook-up apps. Tinder is the most popular…"

I stare at him. "What the fuck?"

"Um, nothin', Pops." He raps me on the back. "Forget I said anything."

I do not want to imagine my daughter doing any such thing. It has me worried.

I know she's been a little wild in her youth, but she's calmed down quite a lot.

We were so proud of Deanna when she went to university and is now building her business in decorating and design. It's slow going, but this town is still relatively small, even with all the recent developments and land sales. Things will pick up. I'm just glad she didn't choose to move to the city.

At that thought, an idea is hitting me fresh in the face.

"Just make sure nothin' happens until we get to the bottom of this." I look through the back window and see Deanna coming toward us.

She opens the door, her face splotchy and eyes bloodshot. I can't reprimand her now, not when she's so upset.

She folds into my arms as I put my hand on the back of her head and kiss the top of it.

"Oh, Dad," she sobs.

I glance at Gears as he winces, then thumbs to the house as he takes off inside.

"It's okay, princess. Mama's gonna be okay. We caught it early."

"Even so, she has to have radiation. Do you know how fucking scary that sounds?"

I hold her close. "Of course I know, but we're gonna all get through this together, you hear me? We will make things a lot easier for Mom around here, starting with you."

She pulls back to look up at me. I brush her tears away with my thumbs.

"What do you need me to do?"

"Why not come stay with us, for a little bit, until Mama starts treatment. She'd appreciate the help."

She bites down on her lip, but nods. "I'd like that. Being back in my old room again."

I smile. "It's settled, then. I'll get your brother to grab your things."

"Dad, I can do that myself."

Shit. Don't cause suspicion.

"Fine. But I don't want you to worry, princess. We're in this together. We'll get through this, okay?"

She nods, but her face is grim.

"Dad?"

"Yeah, sugar."

"Is Mom gonna be okay? Like, really?"

I pull her into a one-armed hug. "Yes. I know it and your mom knows it. You know what I thought when I first saw your momma?"

"You wanted to bend her over?"

I shake my head. "Okay, the second thought." We both laugh. I've made no secret to my kids that I can't keep my hands off my wife. I never have. "How strong-minded she was. At first, she was shy. She didn't really know how to talk to a boy before, much less a biker, but she got more confident as time went on. She got a backbone, and fuck me if I didn't love her even more for it. She put up with some shit from her parents and that made her stronger. It was unfortunate that she had to go through it, but she did. And she came out the other end. She's one tough cookie."

"To be married to you, she has to be."

I squeeze her tight until she squeals. "Dad!"

"Be nice to your old man." I kiss her on the side of the head. "Why don't you grab some stuff and come over tonight. We can have a movie night, get some pizza, and spoil Mom."

She smiles up at me. "That's a good idea." She ruffles my hair, like how I just did to Gears. "When are you gonna cut this?"

"The day you give me grandbabies."

She pulls a face. "Eww, Dad."

I chuckle. "A man can live in hope that he doesn't kick the bucket before he gets at least one to spoil rotten."

"Don't look at me. Go bug Amelia and my brother. They're at it like rabbits. I'm sure it'll only be a matter of time before she's knocked up."

I shake my head. "I guess Gears must take after his old man in that department."

"Oh my God, no," she groans as we head inside. "Can't we have one conversation without you reminding me that you and Mom still have sex. Like that thought isn't gross enough."

"Nothin' gross about it," I retort. "Your mama can't help it if she's still got the goods and knows how to turn my head after all these years."

"Puke, Dad. Seriously."

I let her go and she walks away, shaking her head toward the kitchen where I can hear Kirsty and Gears who often like to cook together.

I do have an ulterior motive to have her home, and I'm not ashamed to admit it.

She can be under my roof for a while until we get to the bottom of this. There was zero hesitation when I suggested she come home. Kirsty won't be starting treatment until early next week, but having Deanna here will make her calmer.

I follow her down the hall, watching from the doorway as Gears throws a handful of flour at Deanna, coating her face and her jet black hair. She retaliates by lobbing the rolling pin at him as they both laugh, wrestling to get the next handful of flour.

Kirsty chastises them, but she laughs too, dodging out

of the way before she gets coated. Meeting my eye, I give her a wink. She smiles.

My baby girl.

I love you, I mouth.

Not as much as I love you, she mouths back.

It has to be okay.

She's the touchstone of this family. Our rock.

I've never needed to be as strong for her as I need to be at this moment.

I'll do anything.

Anything at all to make it better.

BRACKEN RIDGE
REBELS
ARIZONA
M · C

CHAPTER 24

HIASTY

I'm lucky to have such a large family in the club. So many people who care about me.

When Steel pulls me into his massive chest for a hug, I know shit's getting real.

"You feelin' okay, sugar?" I smile when he keeps his meaty arm wrapped around my shoulders.

"Yeah, you?"

"Never better."

They all know, and the one thing I specified I didn't want was a pity party.

I feel a pair of hands snake around my waist. Glancing down at the tattooed hands and skull rings adorning his fingers. I know it's Gunner.

"Hands off, Steel, we all know Mama Bear favors me. Right, Mrs. H?"

"Fuck off," Brock says, pushing him in the chest. "If anythin', Mama Bear loves me the most. I've been here the longest."

I roll my eyes.

I glance around at all my boys; Gears, Bones, Rubble, Axton, Nitro, Colt, Brock, Gunner - who's whispering dirty things in my ear - I arch my neck to look up at Steel, and I feel proud. I feel in some small way I had something to do with the club and how it turned out. And I love it when they call me Mama Bear. They're all like my own children.

"There's plenty of love to go around," I tell them as Gunner shoves Steel's arm away and replaces it with his own.

Gunner hasn't changed all that much. He's still the sunshine in the room, just older now, and still has that aloofness that we all love about him. That little boy Joshua who I remember so well is still in there, but he's come so far since then.

I'm so proud of him, and that he finally admitted his feelings to Lily and they're making a life together.

"Don't stand here too long, or she'll be all over your ass about babies," Bones mutters, but gives me a playful wink as he downs the last of his beer.

"Don't give me the bottom lip," I throw back at him. "You and Kennedy have been together long enough to give me some babies to look after. Growin' old over here."

Gunner's arm tightens around me, as he kisses me on the side of the face. I've always been his Mama Bear, especially now he and Summer's mom lives in Florida and they don't see her as much as they'd like to. I don't play favorites. I love all my boys at the club, but I hold a special place for Gunner, and I always will.

"There she goes again," Bones mutters. "If my woman got any time off to be able to impregnate instead of flittin' off to conferences and shit all the time, then I'd be happy to knock her up and play househusband."

"Wait, you're gonna be a stay-at-home dad?" Colt asks, looking a little bemused.

Bones shoots him a glare. "Yeah? Why not?"

Colt shrugs. "Don't you kinda need to know shit about babies?"

"Shit bein' the operative word," Brock mumbles.

Axton slaps him on the back. "Can't wait to get your helpin' hands when it's time, big brother."

Brock gives him a look. "Does it look like I change diapers?"

"Yes." Rubble laughs. "I've seen you do it a million times. Don't act like you're too fuckin' good for it. Angel would have your ass if you didn't."

Brock shoves him in the side, not even bothering to correct him.

"That's just fuckin' gross," Steel mutters.

"You pick up dog shit, don't you?" Nitro laughs.

"Not if I can help it," Steel replies, looking less than impressed.

"You'll make a wonderful father, Axton," I say as Axton

beams at me. He's so much like Brock in many ways, but also softer. He wears his heart on his sleeve and is so easy to love. Brock, on the other hand, likes to make out he's tough and mean, but I know the real man under the layers. And he's as sweet as they come. A family man. He loves like crazy, but just shows it in other ways. The way he was with Rawlings when he and Angel got back together, it was a sight to behold, and when they had their first baby, Ethan Wolf, it brought something out in him I thought I would never see. Kids definitely change you.

"Would you stop touchin' my mama?" Gears interrupts, pushing Gunner aside and stepping in his place.

"You don't wanna take this outside, do you?" Gunner laughs, shoving him back.

"I've never had so many gorgeous men fighting over me," I snicker. "Kinda makes an old woman feel special."

"You're not old to me, Mrs. H. I'd still go there," Gunner calls, as Gears gets him in a headlock, or tries to.

I shake my head, raising my hands in surrender. "I won't say no."

"She's all talk," says a booming voice from behind me.

The thrill he still gives me.

Hutch.

Peeling Gear's arm from around my shoulders, he steps in his place behind me, putting his arms around my waist. "This one's mine."

"You spoil all the fun," Gunner complains.

Hutch snickers, bringing his mouth to my neck, where he kisses me. My heart still flutters even now, all these years later.

I push my ass back into his groin as he groans.

"Fuck's sake, go get a room," Steel mutters, shaking his head.

"Don't need one, my ol' lady knows beds are for millennials. Right, baby girl?"

"Right." I laugh.

"Nice goin', Pops," Gears says, laughing.

"Don't blame you, Hutch, she's a fine lookin' woman." Nitro grins.

"Hey, Mama Bear, if you need help gettin' in the mood, I've got my new calendar out…" Gunner starts, before Hutch leans across Gears to slap him upside the head.

"My ol' lady knows her Daddy's got what she needs," he growls.

I can't help but laugh. These are my people. My babies. And my man.

"Sorry, boys. Sadly, it is Richie Hutchison who owns my heart…and my body."

"Fuckin' lucky prick," Bones says, giving me a grin.

Hutch nudges me with my hips. "I need you," he whispers. "Now."

"Leaving now will arouse suspicion," I whisper as the boys

start in on Bones for skipping out on his duties at the bar.

"Think I give a fuck? I want them to know I'm gonna go bang my ol' lady on my desk."

I push back against him, feeling his hard cock against my ass. Jesus, this man still does it for me. He always will.

I'm scared, though.

With the radiation.

What if it turns to chemo and my body starts changing. What if my hair falls out?

What if…what if I have to get a mastectomy?

All these things make me shudder.

"Can you take me home?" I whisper.

Sensing the meaning behind my words, he kisses me as I turn my head.

"Yes, my queen."

I lie in his arms. He looks down at me with so much love in his eyes that I want to cry.

I love him so much.

"What was wrong at the club?" he asks, nipping my neck as I bury my fingers in his hair.

"I don't want you to get mad."

He looks up. "I'm listenin'."

"I was thinking…what if…what if stuff starts to

happen…with treatment, you heard what Jenny said. And if we have to start chemo… my hair could fall out…my skin…"

"You wanna discuss this now? While I'm tryin' to fuck you?"

He pushes his cock farther inside me as I let out a breath, then he stills again, seated deep, exactly where I want him.

He does this sometimes. Reminds me I'm his while he makes me wait to come.

It's so damn hot.

My body is on fire for him, like it always is and always will be.

"I'm sorry, you asked."

He lies still, bringing one hand from the mattress to cup my face. "None of that matters. I'll love you till my dyin' day, baby girl, and beyond. None of it means anythin'. You'll always be sexy to me. You know I can't keep my hands off you, I've never been able to."

I smile. "I know that, but I could…I may have to have surgery." Tears spring to my eyes, and I feel so selfish. Worrying about not having breasts when I should be worried about surviving. I'm not vain these days; I keep myself looking my best, and I've had a little bit of Botox to keep the crow's feet at bay, but imagining myself that way, I don't know if I can.

He kisses me long and hard, pulling out and pushing

back in. "Feel that?"

"Yes," I whisper.

"I don't care if you have to have surgery. You're my woman, and I will love you no matter what."

"What if they have to take my breast, or two?"

"Then they take it. I don't care. You're beautiful, baby girl. I will still want you. I'll always want you."

The tears leak. "I just want to be all woman for you, always."

"You are. Your fightin' spirit is what gets me hard. The way you love and let yourself be loved. How everyone you meet is mesmerized by you. How I'm fightin' off fuckin' men half my age because they want to fuck you. You're mine, Kirsty Marie Hutchinson, that ain't gonna change. You're stuck with me."

He wipes away the tears.

"I love you, Richie," I whisper. "I will love you forever.

He smiles, his eyes lighting up. "Those are the only words I ever wanna hear. Now can you shut up so I can hear you call my name while I make you come?"

I giggle as he pulls out and shoves back in, harder. Then he does it again.

And again. And again.

And he sends me to heaven, just like he always does. His body moving over mine as I enjoy every single inch of him.

My beautiful, imperfect, gorgeous man who loves me for who I am.

I don't know how I ever got so lucky.

"Cash?" I say, when I pick up the home phone. "How are you?"

"I'm good, Kirsty. I was wonderin' if Hutch was home. I've tried his cell…"

I glance over at the kitchen table and smile. My husband and technology don't exactly see eye to eye.

"Sorry, Cash. His phone is here with me. I've only just seen it, so he must have left it home again, and it's on silent."

"I'm sorry to hear, Kirsty, about the diagnosis."

"Thank you, that's very kind." I've always liked Cash. He's always been very nice and gracious.

I've never heard him swear in front of a woman, which is rare these days, especially in an MC. He's old school, and I kind of dig that about him. I often wonder why he's never been married, or had anyone permanent in his life. It makes me curious.

I asked him once a long time ago, and he laughed it off. I think something happened and he doesn't like to talk about it. He's a nice-looking man. Fine, actually. Graying nicely at forty-eight, and he keeps himself in good shape. He puts men half his age to shame.

Though he's been friends with Hutch for as long as I can remember, we haven't seen him much over the years, being he's down in New Orleans, running the NOLA Rebels MC. He stopped by only a few months ago on a trip to see his mom who lives in Phoenix. I'd love to see the day when he settles down and perhaps has kids of his own. Of course, I'm baby obsessed. Maybe it's because my own mortality is staring me in the face, I'm not sure. But I'm more clucky now than ever.

"You okay? Hutch treatin' you well?"

"He's smothering me," I admit. "I had to kick him out of the house to get five minutes of peace. I love that he's concerned, but a woman needs her downtime."

"I can imagine. I'm probably gonna be stoppin' by sometime next week, so I just wanted to make sure that was okay.""

"Of course." I beam. "It's no trouble to make up the spare room, though Deanna is staying for the moment, while I have treatment."

"I can stay at the motel. It's not a problem."

"Don't be silly. I insist. Any excuse to cook for someone, and I've been wanting to try out this new recipe for braised lamb chops with mint jelly and baked potatoes."

"A woman after my own heart. Sounds good, Kirst. Is

Hutch at the club? I'll try him there."

"He should be by now. He had some paperwork to catch up on."

"All right, well, you take care. I'll be seein' you soon."

I smile. "Okay, see you next week."

I hang up the phone, and Deanna walks in. "Who was that?"

"Cash," I say, turning to put the kettle on. "He's coming by next week."

Her eyes go wide. "Oh."

"I said he could stay here, if that's okay with you? He'll be in the spare room. That won't be awkward, will it?"

She opens her mouth, then closes it again. Then she shrugs. "It's fine by me."

"Good. Daddy will be happy."

Deanna bites her bottom lip as I narrow my eyes. "What?" I say, taking out the cups.

"Nothing."

"Spit it out."

"I was just thinking about how Summer is going down to New Orleans. I might help her move."

"Oh, that's a good idea."

"But I don't want to leave you, Mom. I wanna be here."

I smile, reaching for the coffee.

"You have to live your life, baby. You can't just be sitting around here, worrying about me. I'm fine. Daddy can come with me anyways, and it's only once a week." The radiation started last week, and I'm doing fine. I'm a little tired at times, but so far, so good.

"I know, but it would only be for a week or two."

"I think you should stay for however long until she's settled. You haven't had a break for a long time. You've been working so hard. When does Summer leave again?"

"She's packing up the week after next."

"I'm gonna miss her."

"Me too." Deanna comes to me and wraps an arm around me. "But I'll miss you if I go."

"You know what will make me really happy, Deanna?" I ask, as she rolls her eyes, knowing I'm about to give her a lecture.

"What? If I hand myself over to a nunnery?"

I laugh. "No. If you settle down and get married, have a couple of kids."

"Mom."

"I'm just saying, nobody knows how long…"

"Ma! Don't start with that shit." She actually sounds angry. "Honestly, just don't."

I turn to her, pushing her long hair back off her shoulders. "I know, I just want so much for you to be happy."

"I am happy."

I smile, knowing that's not true. Maybe in some parts of

her life, but her love life is a disaster. We both know it.

"I want you to find a man who's like your father."

"Old and grumpy?"

I shake my head. "No. A man who loves with all his heart. Who wants what's best for you. Who's there to support you, but lets you have your freedom too. Someone who listens and lets you speak. When you meet the right man, I swear everything will make sense."

"Ma, I don't need a man to be something. And the guy you just described doesn't really exist."

I pull her into a hug, kissing her on the head. "Oh yes, he does, angel, he really does. And when you find him, you'll know. Just like I did with your father."

"God help us," she mutters.

I've no idea what she means, but I chuckle anyway. "I love you. Please make me happy by living your life."

She sighs, not pulling away. "I love you too, Mom. I will, if that's what makes you happy. I'll make you proud."

"You already do."

"Even when I'm a brat?"

"Even then."

"You're the best." She hugs me tighter.

A moment passes. "And babies?" I ask, hopefully.

"Let's not push it."

BRACKEN RIDGE
REBELS
ARIZONA
M · C

CHAPTER 25

HUTCH
ONE WEEK LATER

I hold Kirsty's hand. "You okay?"

She has a million tubes going into her that do not look comfortable. I bought her some romance books to read, the ones with the really good spice that she likes.

All I can do is stare at her, wondering how she's getting through this.

A lump forms in my throat and it won't go away.

She looks up from her book. "I'm fine. Why are you looking at me like that?"

"Like what?"

"Like I'm going to break."

"I'm not. I just wish I could take some of this pain away from you, so you didn't have to bear the load like this."

Her eyes soften. "Baby, I'm lucky. Jenny is positive the cancer hasn't spread, and we will know soon. Until then, I'm going to read this smutty book and dream about the vegan wrap I have waiting for me when we get home."

I've put her on a vegan diet because she needs to be eating whole, organic foods, and red meat isn't favored when you're having treatment like this. I don't even mind them myself. I didn't know you could make tofu taste like anything except rubber. But I've learned that marinade is my best friend.

"Do you need anything?"

"Nope." She looks back down at her book.

"Need to talk," I say.

"We are talking."

"About Deanna."

I've told her about Gears's suspicions, but not to the extent that will worry her, and I didn't wanna do this here.

"Hutch, you're scaring me."

I can't tell her that Gears found a hidden camera, one Deanna didn't know about.

I can't tell her that the guy she hooked up with on Tinder might be the one who planted it there.

I feel fucking sick to my stomach. And the fuckwit is nowhere to be found.

I've decided that Deanna has to get away from here, until the club can sort out this mess.

I don't want her in any danger, and since Summer is moving to New Orleans to finish her nursing degree, I'll be making sure Deanna goes with her.

The only person I trust with my kid and Summer, who

really is like my other daughter, is my best friend, Cash.

I called him last week and he agreed to come out. He knows the situation, and wants to help.

I don't like the idea of Deanna staying at the clubhouse, but Cash has a place adjacent where she can stay and be safe until all of this blows over. All of it will be under the guise of helping Summer move. I just don't know how I'm going to break the news about this whole fuckin' camera business.

How long has this fucker been watching my daughter?

Anger boils up inside me.

"I can't do this here," I say. "I just can't hold it in for much longer."

"Hutch? What's going on?"

"We need to get Deanna away."

"Away where?"

"To New Orleans."

"She is going to help Summer move."

"It may be more permanent."

She stares at me, and I palm the back of my head. I could've waited until her radiation was over. But she's been on at me all morning, knowing I've got something on my mind.

"Why's that?"

I take a long breath. "I think someone has been stalkin' her."

Her eyes go wide with shock. I take both her hands and

rub my thumbs over her knuckles. "I don't wanna go into details, but Gears told me. And it's gonna be okay, baby girl, I'm gonna take care of it."

"Who is it?"

"We don't know. Some guy she was dating briefly."

Kirsty shakes her head. I know my daughter likes to have her fun, as much as that pains me to even think about, but this is beyond anything I'd ever imagined.

The guy's a dead man, whoever he is.

"Holy shit."

"Like I said, he's just become a little bit… over the top, and I think she needs to get away."

"She obviously knows about it, if you say she's being stalked?"

"She had her suspicions." In truth, she doesn't know the heart of it.

"And she didn't tell me?"

"She didn't want to…"

"Worry me?" she whisper-shouts. "Hutch! I'm not going to put up with this. Everyone is sneaking around behind my back, scared I'll break if they say the wrong thing. I'm perfectly capable of learning about something so important, like my own daughter being stalked by a madman!"

I run one hand through my hair. "I said don't get mad at me."

"I'm not. I'm expressing an opinion."

I let that slide. "Baby, I just want to deal with this with the boys, got me? So we need to make sure Deanna stays as long as possible so I can get to the bottom of it. I know she's gonna be worried about you, but it won't be for long."

"I'm fine. I want her safe, Hutch." Tears well in her eyes. "That's all that matters."

"I didn't want to tell you here, but I just…"

She lays a hand on mine. "I know, but I can always tell when you're keeping things from me."

I chuckle, my eyes moving back to hers. "Cash arrives today."

"And he's on board with keeping an eye on her?"

"Of course. He'll do anything I ask of him."

"And Deanna will stay at the clubhouse?" She frowns.

"Cash has a separate residence, so she'll be safe there. Summer will be on campus. I don't want her stayin' in some motel. Cash is family."

She nods, knowing it's the best course of action. "Okay."

"Plus, Cash will keep her busy. He's got some decoratin' and shit he needs takin' care of."

"She'll love that."

"I think it's best."

"You need me to tell her to go, right?"

"Just for the short term, baby. Are you gonna be okay with that?"

"I can go visit, though?"

"We'll see what Jenny says about flyin'."

She nods. "Okay. I'm just…a little shocked."

"Me too, trust me, and Gears ain't happy either. None of the boys are gonna be when I tell them."

There is no rock this little fucker can hide under that I won't find him.

That's my little girl.

I can't bring myself to tell Kirsty the worst of it. I will, but not while she's sitting here, hooked up to a machine. That isn't right. I feel bad enough doing this to her now.

Leaning over, I kiss her gently. "We're in this together, always."

She smiles. "Always, baby."

"Now get back to your book. You always get horny as fuck after readin' those books."

Her eyes go wide as she looks around. It's not like anyone can hear, the nurses are all busy. "Hutch!"

"What? Hey, I don't care where you get inspiration from, baby girl. Long as I'm the lucky recipient."

It pains me to think that Kirsty could ever think I wouldn't want her if her hair fell out or if she needs to have surgery. She's a beautiful soul. The woman I always dreamed of. There is nothing I won't do for her, and my kid.

We're strong, and we will get through this. All of it.

"Oh, you always will be the lucky recipient," she muses,

then raising an eyebrow, she asks, "Is now a good time to discuss handcuffs?"

I smirk. "Atta girl."

Cash sits across from me, looking grave after I told him all we know about Kevin Murphy. The fuckface who's been filming my daughter without her knowledge.

Linc is all over it, but it's gonna take some time to find out where this leads to.

The information we have on him is sketchy. I don't even know if that's his real name.

"How much does D know?"

I look up at him.

"She doesn't know?" he spits. "Fuck, Hutch, you gotta tell her."

"So she'll never feel safe again?"

"No, so she can understand how serious this is."

I roll my eyes. "Clearly, you don't have a daughter."

"If I did, I'd do the same as you, but you said she asked Gears to come stay because she felt like someone was watchin' her, so she does kinda suspect somethin's up."

I look across at my best friend.

He's had a haircut, a little shorter than he usually has it. His gray and white beard is neatly trimmed, and the patch on his cut is old and worn. He's fared well over the years; still gets all the chicks who like the silver fox kink. And he's a good man. His heart is in the right place, but make no mistake, he is the toughest motherfucker I know.

Mess with him and anyone he cares about, you'd better have a helluva good hiding place.

"That's true, but if I tell her about the camera, she's never gonna sleep again."

He rubs his chin, deep in thought.

"That's true, but if you wanna keep her away until you find this deadbeat, then we gotta have a better story."

"Do we have one?"

"I need the entire clubhouse remodeled, rather than just her decoration' and shit. The job would be longer than she anticipated."

My head snaps up. "The entire clubhouse?"

"Have you seen that joint?"

I chuckle. "Not for a while."

"I also got my place to overhaul too. It's in dire need of a paint job and some new flooring. She could arrange all that…guess I better get rid of that stripper pole in my bedroom, though. Don't want her judgin' me."

I shake my head. "Might be a good idea."

He leans forward, resting one arm on my desk. "She'll be safe with me, Hutch. You know that. I'll make sure she's okay, and Summer."

He knows Summer is like a daughter to me. If anything were to happen to either one of them…

"Appreciate it. Thank fuck Summer got moved to your neck of the woods and not fuckin' Cleveland or some shit."

He chuckles. "Thank fuck for small miracles."

There's a knock at my door. "Come in," I say, surprised when Deanna appears.

"Speak of the devil."

She smiles when she sees me, then her eyes flick to Cash. "Oh, sorry, Pops, I didn't know I was interrupting. Hi, Cash."

He half stands as she comes into the room, ever the gentleman.

"Hi, D, how are things?"

"Good," she says, coming over to perch on the side of my desk. "How are you?"

"I'm well, thank you."

"Cash has offered to escort you and Summer to New Orleans," I say, realizing now is as good a time as any to broach the subject. I don't want to say the next part, since I know she'll not be happy…. "And he's also offered to put you up at his place."

She flicks her eyes to Cash's as he looks at her, an unsure look on his face, like he's trying to gauge if this is a good or bad thing he's doing.

She shrugs. "Okay."

I frown. "Just like that?"

She rolls her eyes. "Where else would I be safer if not in a clubhouse full of bikers?"

"Just so we're clear, you're not goin' there to…hook up with anyone…"

Her eyes go round. "Dad!"

"I'm just sayin'…"

She shakes her head, looking at Cash. "Kill me now."

He chuckles. "I'm with your Pops on this one. You'll be safe at the clubhouse, my residence is right behind. I'll let the boys know the rules."

She looks less than impressed with the rules comment, but I know my daughter and her tendency to party. I wouldn't be sending her down there if I didn't trust Cash to take care of her.

"That sounds super serious. Do I have rules too?" she teases. "Curfews and stuff?"

"Absolutely." His tone is firm, and I hide my grin.

If she thinks she can get anything past Cash, she's dreaming.

This trip might be good for her after all.

"Listenin' to Cash is the least of your problems," I add. "We've got a proposition for you."

She rubs her hands together, excitedly. "I'm all ears."

"Well, if you're up for it," Cash begins. "I've got an entire clubhouse to remodel. You've been there for Ryder and Crystal's wedding, so you saw how rundown the place is. It needs an overhaul, of epic proportions."

"Keep talking."

"It'd probably be for a few months, at least."

Her eyes go wide as her excitement fades. "I can't…" She shakes her head. "Mom."

"Your mom knows, and she thinks this would be an amazing opportunity for you," I put in. "And if the doc okays it, we can come visit."

"I don't know, Dad. I really wanted to be with Mom for her treatment."

"I know that, princess, but you still gotta live your life." I can see this will take some convincing. So I add, "Just give it some thought," like she even has a choice.

I know my kid. Making it her decision is the way around making her do anything. Oh, she's going. But if I push her, it'll only make her retreat.

She's a lot like her mama in that way. Stubborn as a mule. Always busting my balls.

I wouldn't want it any other way, though.

"Maybe we can talk over dinner tonight at your parents'," Cash goes on, helpfully. "I can show you some of the more immediate things you could do, and you can give me a quote."

"I'd like that," she says, her voice quiet, like she's deep in thought.

I'll talk to her tonight with Kirsty, when Cash is doing other shit.

I don't want her to know all of the details yet, but she needs to know that shit ain't right with this Kevin fucker. I owe her that much.

I clap my hands together. "It's settled, then."

Cash smiles, lifting to stand at the same time as Deanna. "I better go get unpacked."

Deanna gives me a kiss on the cheek. "See you later, Pops. Cash."

"See you at home, princess." I smile.

Cash gives her a chin lift.

When she's gone, closing the door softly behind her, I say, "I think she'll come without a fight."

Cash watches the door, not so sure. "Hmm, debatable. We've got a few days to work out the details." He points at me. "And you've gotta tell her."

"Already bustin' my balls." I grin, the weight lifting now I know Deanna is gonna be safely away from here.

He smirks. "What are best friends for, old man?"

BRACKEN RIDGE
REBELS
ARIZONA
M.
C

EPILOGUE

KIRSTY

"This is amazing, Kirsty," Cash says, stuffing a mouthful of my newest lamb chop creation in his mouth. "Do you wanna come with D to New Orleans?"

I laugh, happy that he liked it. "I could do with a vacation," I reply, eating my potatoes. "The summers there are pretty rough, though."

Deanna sits next to him. Her eyes find mine, and I know she's conflicted. She's refusing to go for longer than a few weeks. I know once she gets there, and Cash sets her to work, she'll find her feet, and she'll be too immersed in the job to quit.

That's the plan, anyway.

Hutch pats me on the hand as I look up at him. He's been my rock.

Never have I been more in love with him than I am right now. He leans over, and I meet him halfway.

"Ugh, please, Mom and Dad, the kids are at the table."

Deanna complains. "Can we get through one dinner where you two aren't groping one another like teenagers."

Gears chuckles, as does Amelia, who's by his side.

Cash nudges her arm. "Leave them alone. It's nice to see they're still in love after all these years."

She gives him a look. "Ew. You're not the one who has to witness it every day, and on top of that….hear them." She shakes her head. "I'm in the next room, and the walls are paper thin."

I smile, feeling a little embarrassed. Hutch has been extra everything lately, making sure all my needs are met in more ways than one.

"Oops," Hutch says, looking not the least bit sorry. "What can I say? Your mama has always had me right where she wants me."

"What, with handcuffs on?" Gears chuckles.

"Those are for Kirsty," Hutch replies.

Deanna blocks her ears. "Not listening, not listening."

Cash takes another mouthful, chuckling softly to himself. I know he's too old for Deanna…but still, age is just a number…and he's such a nice man…handsome…and single and…no, I can't go there.

He's Hutch's best friend, and he'd never allow it.

But a woman can dream. I meant what I said about Deanna finding a man just like her daddy. Someone who can settle her down and tame her eye. It would be music to my ears to have the right guy take her off our hands.

I chuckle to myself.

Hutch turns to me. "What's so funny?"

I shake my head. "Nothing. I'm just happy."

He smiles. "I'm happy too." He looks down at my plate. "How are your vegan dumplings?"

"They taste like shit."

He laughs wholeheartedly. "And you're still eating them?"

"Anything to make my man happy."

"You know how you can make me happy, baby girl…"

"Pops! For heaven's sake, I get that you can't keep it in your pants when we're here, but we do have company. Can we at least pretend that we're some kind of normal family?" Deanna is yet again disgusted by us.

Cash shakes his head. "I think I've cottoned on a while back, D. There ain't no kinda normal around here."

Hutch points at him. "Got that right."

I link my hand with Hutch's as he opens his palm, looking down the table proudly.

I don't know what the future will hold, but I have hope.

I have all of this love. My family. Those that matter around me who love and care for me. I'm lucky in so many ways. And I've got so much to look forward to.

I won't let this shape me. I will fight this. And having the people I love the most around me makes it that much easier.

My family.

My world.

My everything.

HUTCH
ONE YEAR LATER

"Baby girl?" I call out, setting the flowers down on the table.

I panic when she doesn't greet me. I look in the den, then the study…

"Kirsty?" I bellow.

"In here!" she yells back.

I race to find her, expecting something great since her voice is carrying from the bedroom…and it is our anniversary.

I smile, leaning on the doorjamb when I see her ass in the air…as she's digging through the large chest that holds all her precious things. "You know, when you call a man in that wanton way, next time make sure you have a negligee on."

She turns, smiling at me as she tugs on something in a big, overstuffed suit cover.

Pushing off the door, I go to help her.

I yank it out, dump it behind me, and then pull her back

to my front and kiss her hard when she turns her head. My tongue in her mouth, I let her know that I want sex. Oh fuck, do I want it.

"Baby," she breathes when I pull back. She rubs her sweet ass against my growing cock as I groan. "I thought we were saving that for later?"

I cup her tits. "With a body like this? I don't think so, baby girl."

"So you remembered?"

I laugh. "The day you made me the happiest man in the world?" I rub my nose against hers. "Flowers and chocolates are on the table. I couldn't find you…"

"I was digging something out."

I turn to look over my shoulder. "What is that?"

She giggles like a school kid. "You'll see."

Shooing me away, she turns and picks up the bag, sitting down on the bed as I follow her. She starts to unzip it, and my eyes follow her movements.

I grin. "Is that what I think it is?"

Her sparkling eyes meet mine as she nods. "My wedding dress."

"You still have that?"

She rolls her eyes. "Of course I still have it. I was hoping one day Deanna might…"

I give her a look. "Don't go there."

She smiles wistfully. "Anyway, I just wanted to get it out."

"Put it on."

She shakes her head. "No, it wouldn't fit me now."

"I bet it would. Put it on, then I can fuck you in it, just like I did the night we got hitched."

She rolls her lips. We didn't even wait to get to bed. I couldn't. I was so happy she was mine that we did it around the side of the clubhouse wall. Her dress hitched up around her waist as she rode me. Fuck, those were good times.

She cups my face. "Always a gentleman."

"You know me, baby girl, always tellin' it like it is. In fact, we haven't done it outdoors in forever."

"Hutch, we're in our fifties now."

"So what?"

She shakes her head again. I hold her chin and kiss her again, then I say in a tone that means business, "Put. It. On."

"You drive a hard bargain."

"The only hard thing here is my dick," I say, adjusting my hard-on.

She looks down and bites her bottom lip. Jesus, she drives me over the edge. She always will. I never knew it was possible to love anything or anyone this much.

Especially after thirty-five years together.

I watch as she stands up and starts to undress. Leaning back on my elbows, I enjoy the view as my cock aches to feel her.

Kirsty got the all-clear last week.

No more cancer.

We got it. She had a small surgery to remove a lump, and ongoing radiation, but she's cancer free now. And to see the relief on her face when Jenny told us. I wish I could have that framed.

The future looks bright. She's happy, slowing down at work, only going in twice a week, and only doing showings for the really big clients. Now it's time to enjoy the fruits of our labor and unwind a little bit.

Life is good.

Life is very good.

"Daddy's got something in his pocket," I murmur as she stands in her underwear, bending as she steps into the dress, then slides it up over her body.

She gives me a look. "I think I can see exactly what you have in your pocket."

I rub my chin, chuckling. "Oh, you're gonna get that, baby girl. But I got something else."

She continues to pull the dress up, and I admire how the fabric hugs her curves. It may be a little out of fashion now, but I don't see it that way. Then she does a twirl.

"Like what you see, Mr. Hutchinson?"

"You're so fuckin' hot, Mrs. Hutchinson," I growl.

She leans over, her hand on the box in my left pocket. I wish her hand was covering my cock because it needs relief right now. I lift my hips to help, her hand digging into my jeans pocket and pulling out the box. Her eyes dance with amusement as she shakes her head. "You said nothing elaborate."

"That's because I wanted to outdo you."

She opens the box and gasps. Inside is a big diamond ring with rubies, her favorite stone. "Hutch!" she whisper-shouts in disbelief. "You didn't have to do this."

I pull her between my legs as I sit up. "I wanted to. I want to renew our vows."

Tears start to leak down her cheeks as I wipe them with my thumbs. "You do?"

"Don't sound so surprised."

"Aren't we a little old for that?"

I tsk. "Old isn't even in my vocabulary. Anyway, you keep me fit and young."

"I love you, Richie Hutchison."

I grin. "Not as much as I love you."

She tries it on, holding her hand out as I admire her. "It's beautiful."

"Like you, my queen. Give daddy some sugar."

She cups my face, devouring me as I grip her hips, and she straddles over my lap.

It's then we both hear a huge tear. Oh shit.

She turns, and we both look over her shoulder to see a huge rip in the back near her ass as it hangs out.

I start to shake with laugher, then I throw my head back

and roar, "I guess we better get that fixed."

She slaps me on the chest as I pull the dress up so she can straddle me without ripping it any further. "Stop laughing! This isn't funny! I told you I put on weight." She laughs too, unable to contain it.

"You look perfect to me. Then again, you always do. Especially when you're indecent."

She throws her arms around my neck. "Are you just trying to get lucky, Mister? You know I'm married."

"Yes, and your husband is a jealous, greedy son of a bitch."

"He is?"

"Yes, and he's got a big fat cock because you're rubbin' yourself on me, and I'm gonna explode in a minute."

"Hmm, just like old times."

"I'll give you old." We kiss again, my heart pumping ten to the dozen because this is exactly how she makes me feel, and always will. I'm forever young.

She sighs. "I'm so glad you almost spilled your coffee on me."

I chuckle. "You almost made me spill the coffee. All these years together, and we still can't agree on that."

And this is how we will be, for always.

Our chapter will live on, and so will our story, forever.

She's the flame that will never burn out. She's the light in my life, my heart, my world. I will never, ever take anything for granted, not when she's made me this happy.

It's more than I could ever hope for. More than a guy like me deserves.

She kisses me chastely. "Never. Where's the fun in agreeing on everything?"

"Touché," I mutter, my lips finding hers again. "You may be my baby girl, but you'll forever be my queen."

THE END

ACKNOWLEDGMENTS

Wow it's been a wild ride. The last Bracken Ridge full length book!!! Who'd have thought that we'd come this far after my little book Steel was released in lockdown of 2020 and now I'm a full-time author with 11 books in the series!? And I have YOU guys, my readers, to thank for it. I have no words. Just know how eternally grateful I am to all of you for all of your love and support. I'm so proud of this series, it's been close to my heart for so many years and it's gotten me through some seriously tough times.

I hope to keep writing more stories for you for many years to come.

To my sister D, thank you for being my number one cheerleader and champion. I'm glad I have you to vent to because you've had 3 years of it with this series LOL

Thank you to my fabulous Alpha reader Michelle and Beta readers Alana, Kate and Jennifer for all that you do and for all your help making me a better writer.

Thank you, Kiki, for proofreading and picking up all of the things I change last minute that makes absolutely no sense, phew! Glad I got you girl!

To my amazing PA Alana @thenovelassistant. Words can't express how grateful I am for all of your help, assisting me at my first signing this year and being totally amazing. Love ya guts x

Thank you to Savannah and the team @ PeachyKeen author services for my blog tours and amazing graphics!

Hugs to my editor Mackenzie @nicegirlnaughtyedits for all that you do and for not getting cross at me when I use the same word fifty thousand times.

Thank you to my amazing ARC team for your continued support and wanting my books

Thank you to the new and existing blogger ARC's who signed up to read and review, your honest reviews are much appreciated!

Thanks LJ from Mayhem Cover Creations for the great cover design

Thank you to Crown Designs for the cover picture for Hutch – he is perfect!

If you can spare the time to leave a review on GR and/or Amazon if you loved Hutch or any of my books that would be greatly appreciated and helps me so much as an indie author. Links are on the following pages.

I have news about what's next, you may be pleasantly surprised…info below…

Be sure to check out my private Facebook group (links below) as I update this page regularly before anything gets released on other social media channels.

Love from Australia, MF xx

FIND ME AT

Facebook: https://www.facebook.com/mackenzy.foxauthor.5

Instagram: https://www.instagram.com/mackenzyfoxbooks/

Tiktok: https://www.tiktok.com/@mackenzyfoxauthor

Linktree: https://linktr.ee/mackenzyfox

Goodreads: https://bit.ly/2TKp7ck

https://books2read.com/Steel-BRR

Website: https://mackenzyfox.com

Join my private Facebook group for all the juicy gossip, giveaways and spicy reveals first at The Den - A Mackenzy Fox Reader Group - https://bit.ly/3dgQfKk

ABOUT THE AUTHOR

Mackenzy Fox is an author of contemporary, romantic and erotic themed romance novels. When she's not writing she loves vegan cooking, walking her beloved pooch's, reading books and is an expert on online shopping.

She's slightly obsessed with drinking tea, testing bubbly Moscato, watching home decorating shows and has a black belt in origami. She strives to live a quiet and introverted life in Western Australia's North West with her hubby, twin sister and her dogs.

ALSO BY MACKENZY FOX

Bracken Ridge Rebels MC:
Steel
Gunner
Brock
Colt
Rubble
Bones
Axton
Nitro
Gears
Knox

Medici Mafia:
Fortress of the King
Fortress of the Queen
Fortress of the Heart
Fortress of the Soul
Fortress of the Damned
Fortress of the Brave

Bad Boys of New York:
Jaxon

Standalone:
Broken Wings